THE DIAMOND ROSARY MURDERS

An enthralling crime mystery full of twists

ROGER SILVERWOOD

Yorkshire Murder Mysteries Book 19

JOFFE BOOKS

Revised edition 2020
Joffe Books, London
www.joffebooks.com

First published in Great Britain 2012

Please join our mailing list for free Kindle books and new releases.

www.joffebooks.com/contact

We love to hear from our readers! Please email any feedback you have to: feedback@joffebooks.com

ISBN: 978-1-78931-540-0

ONE

Chief Officer's office, Senford Open Prison, Suffolk.
Friday, 5 August 2011. 7.45 a.m.

'Come in, Paschal,' Chief Officer Wainwright called.

The big man with the black beard came into the office and closed the door.

Chief Officer Wainwright was seated at his desk. He rubbed his chin and looked up at the man.

Paschal pulled a weary face and said, 'Is this for the regular, goodbye lecture about being a good boy, when you tell me that I have been honoured to be given another chance to be let out on the great, good world and that you don't want to see me back here again?'

Wainwright's knuckles tightened. 'Sit down, Paschal, and listen. You might *learn* something.'

Paschal seemed to be considering whether to obey the order or not. Eventually he slumped down heavily into the chair.

Wainwright continued. 'You seemed to have tolerated the regime here well enough. You are an educated man, let's hope it has given you time to reflect upon your life and the reasons why you are here.'

'Oh yes, sir. It's a great place. I shall commend it to the RAC. They might give it a couple of stars.'

Wainwright's face muscles tightened. 'What's the smart lip for, Paschal? What's the matter with you? You're being released today. You should be very pleased to get out of here.'

Paschal sighed. He looked down at the floor briefly and then he looked up. His mood had changed. The bravado had gone. He spoke quietly. 'I don't know, Mr Wainwright, I am all mixed up. I haven't any money nor any work to go to. Employment prospects are bleak and they'll be even harder for me in my job. My ex-wife has possession of what *was* my house — I won't be welcome back there. I haven't actually anywhere permanent to go.'

Wainwright looked up from the file open in front of him and said, 'It says here you're going to stay with your sister in Nottingham.'

'Huh. That's right. Only for a couple of nights or so. Her husband won't want me under his feet for long, and who could blame him?'

'Hmm, well, you'll have a railway warrant, enough subsistence to provide for accommodation and food until your first appointment with your Probation officer. Whatever Probation can't provide, you can go the local council, alternatively . . .'

'I know all that stuff, sir.'

'I suppose you do, Paschal. I suppose you do.'

Paschal's eyes flashed. He sat bolt upright. 'This was only my *third* offence, Mr Wainwright, and it wasn't my fault.'

The prison officer's nose turned up. 'Maybe. Maybe not. But don't give me that,' he said. 'You *all* blame somebody else. You've got to keep away from bad company, lad,' he said, then he closed the file on his desk. 'Anyway, we could argue all day and you're due out in ten minutes. Look lad, you've been a model prisoner here. Matron says you've been a first-rate sick bay orderly, and the doctor has given you a good report at dispensing the pills. Not so much as an aspirin unaccounted for. I hope you will be a model citizen out there and make a go of it?'

'I want to, Mr Wainwright.'

'Well, I certainly hope you do,' Wainwright said. He stood up and held out his hand. 'Good luck, lad.'

They shook hands warmly. 'Thank you, Mr Wainwright. Thank you very much.'

'And don't come back.'

Bromersley, South Yorkshire, UK.
Tuesday, 6 December 2011. 7.55 p.m.

Detective Superintendent Horace Harker and his wife were at home watching television. The old French wall clock said the time was exactly 7.55 p.m. The policeman wrinkled his nose, turned to his wife and said, 'Got to go out now. Won't be long.'

She frowned then said, 'Right, dear.'

Horace Harker was the Detective Superintendent and second in command at Bromersley Police Station. Such a position brought with it certain perks and privileges, but also the occasional sacrifice. That night was such an occasion. He was leaving *Bad Girls*, without knowing whether the villainous woman in the prison riot survived the beating from the equally villainous male prison officer or not. And he wasn't pleased.

He picked up the jar of Vicks and a wodge of Kleenex from the side table and stuffed them into his pocket. Then he ambled into the hall, put on his scarf, overcoat and hat, and opened the front door of the semi-detached bungalow on Pine Avenue, off Creesforth Road. The freezing air met his warm cheeks causing a shiver to run up his skinny spine. He blinked several times, closed the bungalow door and turned round into the cold night.

The sky was as black as fingerprint ink.

He brushed past the Cupressus bush glimpsing a wisp of fog gliding through it. The corners of his mouth turned downwards, he frowned then gave an involuntary cough. Venturing forth into the cold at night did not suit his chest nor his temperament. He pulled the scarf over his mouth.

He was answering an unusual letter that had been pushed through his letterbox requesting — nay summoning — him, to call on Haydn King, of the King's Breweries empire, at his home that evening at eight o'clock. The letter had also said that it was on an urgent matter of confidential police business, and it instructed him to bring the letter with him.

Normally under such circumstances, on a winter's night like that, Harker would have shredded such a missive, put on his slippers, embraced a hot-water bottle, sucked on a cube of sugar dosed with drops of Friar's Balsam and watched *Bad Girls* on the television with his wife all the way to its mesmeric conclusion. But not tonight. Haydn King was not a man to be ignored. He was not some small-time nonentity the superintendent could have pushed quietly to one side: King was immensely rich and powerful.

The two men had not met, even though they lived opposite each other on select Pine Avenue. Last summer, when Harker was cutting his hedge, King's Rolls Royce had slowed and stopped to permit the remote-controlled gates to his mansion to open, and during those seconds, Harker had caught a glimpse of the bearded man in the back seat of the car, with the sour face poring over a document, while constantly picking, stroking, pulling and generally examining his ample beard as if he was a rodent searching for crumbs. Tonight, however, it would be different. He was to meet and converse with the great man face to face.

Harker crossed the narrow lane. There was no traffic at all in that quiet backwater at that hour. He saw that the electronic gates to King's mansion were open. They had always been shut. They must have been opened specifically to allow him to enter. He set off up the long drive, that twisted elegantly one way and then another through an acre or two of lawn, past a screen of evergreen bushes and trees and round to the front of the big stone edifice. There was a solitary powerful light visible through the fog. He made his way towards it. It illuminated the big stone entrance to the front door. He climbed the three steps and before he could touch the bell push, the door opened and a fully liveried man in his fifties looked out at him.

'Good evening, sir. Can I help you?'

'Mr Haydn King has asked me to call on him. My name is Detective Superintendent Harker.'

'Yes, indeed, sir,' the man said. 'Mr King *is* expecting you. Please come in. May I take your coat?'

Harker lifted his nose to sense the temperature of the hall. Surprisingly it felt comfortably warm, so he began to unfasten the buttons.

A clock chimed eight o'clock.

'My name is Meredith, sir. I am Mr King's butler.'

Harker sniffed then nodded.

Meredith assisted him with the coat, showed him to a comfortable chair in an alcove near the door. 'Mr King won't keep you a moment, sir,' he said. 'Can I get you any refreshment?'

'No, thank you,' Harker said.

Meredith nodded politely, then took the coat down the long hall through a door and disappeared.

Harker looked round. He noticed the brass-faced grandfather clock opposite showing the exact time. He looked up at the dozen or so large old oil paintings on the walls, mostly portraits of elderly men in wigs, occasionally with women, children or dogs. The paintings almost covered the walls. He glanced upward at the high-vaulted timber and plaster ceiling, and the wide staircase.

He settled back in the chair and rested his eyes. He heard a distant door close and footsteps approach. He glanced at the clock and it was four minutes past eight.

The footsteps belonged to Meredith. He came right up to Harker and in a quiet voice said, 'Sorry to have kept you waiting, sir. Mr King will see you now.'

Harker stood up, and Meredith went up to the door nearest to them and tapped on it.

'Come,' a loud voice said.

Meredith opened the door into a big, shadowy room with books all round the walls. The only light was from a small powerful lamp in the centre of the huge desk. Seated at the desk was a big man in a Reid & Taylor suit, and with an elegant black beard and spectacles. On the desk in front of him, piled high, were books, ledgers and papers of all kinds. He was reading something when they entered and he didn't immediately look up.

Meredith led Harker to a chair this side of the desk, and Harker sat down.

Meredith returned to the door and standing erect, in his best Shakespearian voice, said, 'Detective Superintendent Harker, sir.'

'Right, Meredith,' the big man said, waving him away.

Meredith left the room, closing the door quietly.

'Did you bring the letter I wrote to you, Superintendent?' the big man said.

Harker took the letter in its envelope out of his inside pocket and passed it across the desk.

The man reached out for it.

Harker's eyebrows raised slightly when he noticed that the man took it out of its envelope, glanced at it then tossed it to one side on his desk.

The man leaned back in his chair. His face was out of the glare of the desk lamp. He began to rub his chin and pick at his beard. 'Now then, Superintendent,' he began. 'I have a strange tale to tell. Firstly, I want you to understand that I am a man of some substance. I founded and built up the King brand of beers and lagers, which now sell all over the UK and seventeen countries abroad. I am chairman of the company which is now a PLC, and the stock market valuation is over two hundred and fifty million pounds. I have been married and divorced. I have no children. I have travelled all over the world, executed business with all kinds of people. My own physician tells me that I am sound in body and mind. I swim more than twenty-four lengths most days. I don't smoke. I drink very little. I don't take drugs. And I am not on any prescribed medication. Right?'

'Right, Mr King,' Harker said. 'Are you going to tell me—'

'I am coming to the point, Superintendent,' he said. 'Every night, for this last two weeks or so, when I have finished here, I go upstairs. Get undressed. Get into bed and go straight to sleep. At some early hour of the morning, I have the strangest experience. I dream that I waken up. I go downstairs to the swimming pool, take off my night attire, put on my trunks, dive into the pool, eventually rise to the surface of the water to find that I am dead. However, somehow I manage to see my dead body still there floating in the water. I look down at the dead man as if it is somebody else, but no, it is *me*. I begin to shake and shudder, and feel as if I want to vomit. I cannot bear to look at my own body dead in the water. Right?'

'Right,' Harker said.

'Well, what do you think to that, Superintendent?'

Harker frowned. After a few moments he said, 'Is *that* the matter you wanted to speak to me about, Mr King?'

'Yes. Of course it is,' he snapped.

Harker blinked several times. 'Well, sir,' he began, rubbing his chin. 'How do you waken in the morning? *Where* are you?'

'In bed, of course.'

Harker sighed, then slowly said, '*Safely* in bed? Is nothing in the bedroom disturbed?'

The man's eyes glowed like a cat's in headlights. He stared hard at the policeman. 'Don't tell me it's just a dream. It is far too vivid. And it is repeated each night in such detail. I see myself floating face down in the pool. It is *me*. *My* body. I am *dead*! Something strange is happening.'

'You need a doctor,' Harker said. 'Or maybe a holiday. Or both.'

The big man thrust his arms up in the air in anger.

'I need more than that,' he roared. 'The fantasy is too vivid. I have dreamt it too often to ignore it any longer. There must be a reason for it. Can you not solve the mystery then?'

Harker shook his head.

'You're a detective, aren't you? What should I do? Have you nothing useful to say? Can you not solve the puzzle?

Have you no explanation? Can't you suggest what I might do?'

Harker continued shaking his head. 'I am sorry, Mr King, this is not a police matter. I am afraid not, sir.'

The man leaned forward onto the desk and stuck his thumb on a button push, one of several, and held it on. At the same time he stared hard at Harker and said, 'You are useless. Get out. Get out. What do I pay my taxes for? Get out!'

Harker stood up, his face as red as a judge's robe. 'This is preposterous,' he said. 'Outrageous. This is not the way to speak to a Superintendent of Police. If you have no respect for me, you should at least have respect for the force.'

The door opened. It was the butler, Meredith.

'The superintendent is leaving,' the man roared and returned to the papers on his desk.

Harker wondered what to reply.

Meredith took in the scene. He stood by the open door trying not to catch Harker's eyes.

'*Immediately*,' the man added, waving an arm.

Harker stamped out of the room.

Meredith closed the door. He produced Harker's coat from a nearby chair and held it up for him to put on. 'I hope Mr King hasn't upset you too much, sir.'

Harker's breathing was heavy and laboured. He didn't reply. He tucked in his scarf and yanked on his leather gloves.

Meredith opened the front door.

'Goodnight, sir.'

Harker looked out at the cold, foggy blackness. His heart was still beating heavily. He lifted his coat collar, pulled his scarf across his mouth and stepped outside.

Hatton Garden, London, UK.
Wednesday 7 December 2011. 11.00 a.m.

It was just another working Wednesday in the jewellery centre of the UK. There was the constant, busy hum of city traffic. Young men with briefcases dashed along the pavement into cars and taxis. Doors slammed. Engines revved up and were quickly driven away. Old men with long beards, wearing large black overcoats, Homburgs and white shirts stood around here and there, looking nowhere at all. Women and girls carrying shopping and sandwiches made their way purposely along the pavement eager to get out of the cold December wind.

Suddenly from the ground floor of a building, an alarm bell began to ring and a light above it flashed intermittently. A cloud of pigeons fluttered upwards. Seconds later, another bell at the side of the same building began to ring. The two bells created an insistent racket. Some people stopped momentarily and looked up at them. Others scurried away. Then there was an explosion, the sound of breaking glass and splintering wood. That was followed by another explosion. Then a door at the side of the building flew open and in a cloud of smoke a woman with a shock of blonde hair and a scarf over her mouth, and a big man clutching something under his arm, came running down an alley. A big silver Mercedes Benz arrived from nowhere and jerked to a stop, its rear passenger door hanging open. The man and the woman rolled into it. The door slammed shut. The driver hit the accelerator and the powerful engine roared into life. With a squeal of tyres, the car rocked down Greville Street and turned left onto Farringdon Road.

About a hundred metres up the road, the car slowed then stopped at a dishevelled-looking newspaper-seller on the pavement at the side of the road. He had a canvas newspaper bag with the words *London Chronicle* printed in red over his shoulder and hanging down by his waist, and a bundle of papers under his arm.

'Paper, please,' the man in the car said.

The paper-seller came unusually close to the side of the car. '60p, Guv,' he said. Then he glanced to his right and to his left, and then opened wide the bag half-filled with newspapers. The man in the car leaned out of the open window and dropped something into it as the paper-seller handed him a paper from under his arm. The sleight of hand took only a split second.

The paper-seller promptly closed the bag, and in a loud voice said, 'Thank you, Guv.' Then he turned away from the car and began to hobble at speed back along Farringdon Road.

The man in the car pressed the button to close the window, as the Mercedes roared away up towards the busy junction; it was soon lost in London traffic.

Minutes later Hatton Garden was swarming with police cars and policemen. Three hours after that, the headline of the *London Chronicle and Advertiser* read:

> *DARING HATTON GARDEN ROBBERY. BLOODY MARY'S £20M GEMSTONE ROSARY STOLEN. £1M REWARD OFFERED.*

At 10.55 a.m. today, thieves raided the showroom of Julius Henkel Limited, antique jewellery dealer of Hatton Garden, London. Police say that it was probably the work of the Chameleon, however it is not known whether he took any active part in the raid. The armed robbers used grenades and handguns.

A man came into the showroom with a blonde woman, whom he introduced as his wife; he gave his name and address which appeared to be that of a genuine jewellery dealer and his wife from Glasgow. The couple purported to be interested in purchasing, on behalf of a syndicate, the fabulous diamond-and-ruby Rosary given by King Philip II of Spain to Mary I, Queen of England, on the occasion of their wedding on 25 July 1554.

Julius Henkel, chairman of the company, said the Rosary was unique and comprised a gold crucifix with all the beads represented by precious stones, mostly diamonds, and every decade a ruby, all threaded onto a gold chain. The presentation of the Rosary was made at Kensington Palace on 23 July 1554. The marriage took place two days later. The Rosary was in a brown leather presentation case.

The leader of the gang who did all the speaking in what was thought to be a Scottish accent was portly, aged about fifty, had dark hair, a moustache and beard, horn-rimmed spectacles, and wore a dark suit. His accomplice was a woman aged thirty-five years who had a 'striking' figure, long blonde hair, and was wearing a dress decorated with black lace and a matching coat. The third man was the driver of the car which was said to be a silver Mercedes. The licence plate was found to be false.

A witness said that he saw a car thought to be the getaway car stop to buy a newspaper from a street vendor on Farringdon Road.

There is a reward of £1m for information leading to the capture and identity of the Chameleon and the return of the jewel.

TWO

The King George Hotel, Bromersley, South Yorkshire.
Wednesday 7 December 2011. 10.30 p.m.

James Argyle was the first into the room. His arms were behind his back and bound at the wrists with brown sticky parcel tape.

Behind him, pushing him, was Charles Domino. He had the barrel of a Walther 38 sticking into Argyle's spine. He jabbed it into him meanly from time to time.

'All right. All right,' Argyle said in a crisp Scottish accent.

Domino looked down his nose at him and said, 'I just don't want you to forget who is running this show.'

Argyle looked round the shabby hotel bedroom. He wrinkled his nose as if he'd just caught a whiff of the gravy vat in the cookhouse at Strangeways.

'Not exactly the Ritz,' he said.

'It's good enough for you,' Domino said. He waved the Walther in the direction of a chair placed strategically at the far side of the room. 'Sit over there,' he said, pushing him by the shoulder.

Argyle staggered towards the chair. 'Steady on. Who are you, anyway? What do you want? And where's my wife?'

'She's not your wife. She wouldn't marry a tub of lard like you,' Domino said as he moved behind the chair.

'She'd better be all right. I don't like that smelly, foreign little turd of yours hanging round her. Besides, *she* can't tell you anything. She doesn't *know* anything.'

'Anything about *what*?'

'Anything about anything. Tell me what you want and let me get out of this rat hole.'

Argyle peered round to see what Domino was doing behind him.

'Look to your front,' Domino snapped, jabbing the barrel of the gun into Argyle's right kidney.

Domino produced a length of rope, draped it over Argyle's front, pulled it round the back, threaded it through the chair spindles, pulled it tight and fastened it with a double knot.

'Where is she, anyway?' Argyle said. 'She'd better be all right.'

'Never mind *her*,' Domino said, coming round to his front. He pulled two more short pieces of rope out of his pocket and fastened each of Argyle's ankles round a chair leg.

Argyle tried to move his legs but couldn't. He sighed.

Domino smiled.

Argyle's eyes narrowed. Events were moving too fast for him. He had had no time to think things out. He was used to meticulous planning, weighing the risks, considering possibilities and options: this was not one of them. He licked his bottom lip with the tip of his tongue. He was in a mess. He tried to alter the position of each leg and then his arms. He could manage very little movement. The muscles of his face tightened. 'What's all this about?' he said.

Domino stuffed the Walther in his pocket, pulled out another chair, placed it in front of him back to front, about a metre away and sat astride it.

Argyle was angry, and he was also afraid. He looked up at Domino and said, 'What *are* you doing? Who *are* you and what do you want?'

There was a knock at the door. It comprised three quick taps, a pause and then a single tap. Domino got up, crossed the room, pulled out the Walther and unlocked the door.

A woman almost fell in. Her arms were behind her back and her wrists also tied with brown sticky tape. She had a shock of blonde hair, and a figure with more curves in it than Silverstone. She was wearing a black lace dress and matching coat. Her eyes seemed to be half closed, and she had a permanent pout.

She was pushed in roughly by a small man in a smart double-breasted suit.

The man was Joseph Memoré. He was foreign-looking, had a face like a frog, and a smile like a snake. Memoré was perspiring a lot and had big, piercing blue eyes.

Argyle's face was red. He looked across at her. 'Are you all right, Marcia?'

She looked at Memoré as if he was something you wipe off your shoe after a walk in the park, then bawled out, 'Yeah. Yeah. I'm all right.'

'If that little foreign turd has as much as touched you . . .'

Memoré's eyes shone like lasers and his face reflected perspiration. He began breathing heavily. He quickly dived into his pocket and took out a small, blue Beretta handgun. He ran across to Argyle, waved the pistol under his nose and said, 'You annoy me, Argyle,' in a strained, high-pitched voice. 'Just keep quiet, otherwise I may have to do somesing about it.'

Argyle looked him in the eye. He said nothing. It was not a good idea to argue with a man with a gun pointing at you.

'Anybody got a cigarette?' Marcia Moore said in a voice that sounded as if she was about to drop off to sleep.

Domino glared at Memoré and said, 'All right, Joseph. Don't get so excited.'

'I could *keel* him,' Memoré said.

'All right. All right. Keep calm. What about *her*?' Domino said.

'She says she knows nossing.'

Marcia glanced round the room again. 'Anybody got a cigarette?' she said.

Domino placed a chair next to Argyle's, looked at Marcia and said, 'Sit here.'

She crossed the room like a cat and obediently made her way to the chair.

Memoré watched her sit down and cross her legs and smiled. He liked looking at her legs. When he smiled, he looked as if he was about to vomit.

Domino took up a position astride the chair facing Argyle.

'You robbed Henkel's today and got away with the Rosary worth twenty million.'

A slow smile developed on James Argyle's whiskered face. 'I should be so fortunate, my good man,' he said.

'I want it,' Domino said. 'Or rather the Chameleon wants it.'

On hearing the mention of the Chameleon, Argyle's eyes opened wide.

Everybody was scared of the Chameleon. Where there was anything worth stealing, the Chameleon was there. He murdered anyone who got in his way. He slipped a slim knife between his victim's ribs into the heart, and death was instantaneous. It took only two seconds. And it was an amazing fact that nobody knew who he was.

Both Domino and Memoré saw Argyle's reaction. They were not surprised.

Memoré came across to the Scotsman, waving the Beretta in his face again. 'I vant it too,' he said. 'Don't mess about, Argyle.'

'It has your stamp on it, Jimmy,' Domino said. 'Don't waste time denying it.'

'I don't know anything about it,' Argyle said. '*And don't call me, Jimmy*!' he bellowed.

Memoré looked at the Scotsman. He didn't like what he saw. The little man rubbed his chin.

‘Marcia and I were in Meadowhall at the time of the robbery,’ Argyle said. ‘You’re confusing us with another couple. Isn’t that right, Marcia?’ he said, turning to her.

She shrugged and continued looking down at the carpet. Her eyes appeared to be closed. ‘Guess so. Anybody got a cigarette?’

Memoré suddenly breathed in noisily, raised himself to his full height of 5’ 2”. He seemed to have made a decision. He was clearly excited. His eyes were shining. He was almost smiling. ‘Let’s do it, Charles. Dis is only so much a vaste of time. Let’s get on with it.’

Argyle looked at Memoré and frowned. He wondered what it was they were to get on with.

Domino looked back at Memoré and said, ‘Let’s give him a chance.’

Memoré’s face tightened. He was not pleased. ‘It’s just so much a vaste of time,’ he said with a shrug.

Domino looked back at Argyle and said, ‘We want to be reasonable about this, Jimmy. Where is the Rosary? Where is it?’

Argyle’s eyes opened wide. ‘I haven’t got it,’ he said. ‘I have never had it. I don’t know anything about it. I can’t be more explicit than that.’

‘Where did you go after you left Hatton Garden?’

Argyle looked weary. ‘We didn’t go *anywhere*. We weren’t in Hatton Garden.’

‘You called in at Harry’s to have the number plates changed.’

Argyle’s head swivelled round. That *had* touched a nerve. It had been a closely guarded secret part of Argyle’s plot.

Harry’s was a one-man business situated in a lock-up contrived from space under an arch of the main railway line from St Pancras to Birmingham New Street. It was a specialist drive-in place — not open to the general public — where Harry Polinger would supply and change number plates on the spot and at great speed for a fee. The faster, the dearer.

Argyle frowned. How could Domino have known that?

'The job was done at 12.30,' Domino continued. 'After you called at Harry's, then at Newton Pagnell for a turkey sandwich and a cup of black coffee.'

There were more shocks on Argyle's face.

Domino smiled. 'You see you were monitored the whole time, my dear James.'

Argyle stared at him.

'From the moment you put on your wee tartan socks this morning,' Domino said, 'until the moment we picked you up on the M1 this afternoon. So this babbling that you weren't down the garden lifting the Rosary from Henkel's is just so much hot air.'

Memoré strutted up to Argyle, waving the gun again. 'This whole sing is a vaste of time. So vere have you put the Rosary?' he said. 'We want it and we will get it.'

Argyle shook his head slightly. He froze when he saw Memoré out of his eye corner. Beads of perspiration appeared on the Scotsman's forehead.

Domino's facial muscles tightened. 'For the last time, Argyle,' he said, 'where is the frigging Rosary?'

Memoré stood there, a face like Krakatoa, in his small bespoke suit, arms by his sides, Beretta in his pocket, looking as smart and efficient as a hypo of cyanide. He clenched and unclenched his fists twenty times.

Argyle looked straight ahead.

Memoré said, 'Come on, Charles. Let's do it. Let's start with *heem*.'

Domino looked at the Scotsman. 'Do you know what floor this is, Mr Argyle?' he said.

Argyle gave a little shrug. He didn't know and he didn't care.

'I'll tell you. We are on the fifth floor. The *fifth* floor.'

Argyle looked straight ahead.

'If you open the window,' Domino said, 'you'll see it's a long way down.'

Memoré's eyes lit up. 'Yes. Yes,' he said excitedly and rushed over to open it. A cold breeze blew into the room.

The cold air made Marcia Moore look up. She peered at the open window and shivered.

Argyle looked straight ahead, feigning indifference. He couldn't see the window. His chair had been placed at the other end of the room and the old chimney breast cut off his direct view of it. The chimney itself had been bricked up, plastered over and covered with distemper many years ago.

Marcia Moore had been following what was happening on and off, and had looked progressively more uncomfortable. 'Has anybody got a cigarette?' she said.

The three men looked at her.

'What's going on?' she said. 'Shut the window. It's cold.'

Domino turned to her. 'There you are, Marcia. I thought we had lost you entirely. Your boyfriend has conveniently lost his memory. He refuses to tell us where the Rosary is.'

'Well I don't know where it is,' she said, 'I've already told you that.'

'Yeah, so *he* is going out of the vindow,' Memoré said, smiling. His eyes shone like the headlights on the Chief Constable's Mercedes. 'The fresh air might bring back de memory.'

Argyle and Marcia Moore's eyes met.

Argyle said, 'Don't be ridiculous, man. You can't do that.'

'We can,' Domino said, his patience now entirely exhausted. He jumped up and looked across at Memoré who smiled and nodded.

'We can. *We can,*' Memoré said. There was an unmistakable sense of triumph in the foreigner's voice. He advanced on Argyle.

Domino threw his chair angrily out of the way. It clattered and rattled and ended upside down in the corner of the room.

Argyle swallowed, then stared at them in astonishment.

Domino went down on one knee and began to unfasten a tie round one of his ankles.

Argyle looked down at him. 'What's happening? You're not seriously intending to—'

'You don't mean it,' Marcia said. 'You're out of your mind.'

Memoré's fists tightened. He glared across at her. 'Vee are not out of minds,' he bawled. 'Just tell us what you have done with the Rosary. That's all you have to do.'

Argyle said, 'She doesn't know. Leave her alone. If you harm her, you will pay for it.'

Memoré sniggered. He turned to Domino and said, 'Let's throw *her* out first.'

Domino looked up. His forehead creased in thought. He looked across at her and made the decision. He retied the rope round Argyle's ankle then stood up.

Marcia Moore gasped.

Memoré smiled, his face as repulsive as the smell and sight of the steamed cod on the hotplate in Strangeways cookhouse. He dashed over to Marcia Moore, took hold of one arm and pulled her to her feet. Domino took hold of the other arm.

'You can't do this,' Argyle said. 'This is murder.'

'You're the murderer,' Domino said. 'You know how to stop it.'

Argyle stared resolutely ahead.

Domino and Memoré dragged Marcia Moore across the room to the window. The toes of her shoes dragged across the carpet.

'You can't do this,' she said.

They lifted her out through the window.

'No. No. *No*!' she said.

Her legs dangled over the side of the sill.

'James! *James!*' she cried. 'If you have any pity in you at all, James, tell them where it is.'

Argyle's eyes grew bigger than fried eggs in a pan.

Domino said, 'This is your last chance, Argyle. *Where is the Rosary*?'

Argyle swallowed.

'Let her go, Charles,' Memoré said. 'I vant to see her fly.'

'No,' Marcia screamed weakly. 'You can't do this. Please. Please don't do this. James! James, help me!'

Domino's face was scarlet. '*Where is the Rosary*, Argyle?' he yelled.

Argyle stared ahead as if in a trance.

'I can't hold her any longer,' Memoré said. 'Let her go.'

There was the slightest gasp from Marcia Moore and she was gone into the cold, dark night.

Memoré's eyes glowed like a cat's caught in headlights. 'Just look at that,' he said with a smile. 'Vonderful.'

The two men came back from the window. They stared at Argyle. His lips were trembling.

Memoré rushed to a suitcase under the bed, opened it, found a torch and went back to the window. He looked out and flashed the torch down below briefly. 'You should look at this, Mr Argyle.'

The Scotsman was in a daze.

Domino and Memoré unfastened the ties round his legs and waist and escorted him across the room to the window. All three men stuck out their heads. Memoré flashed the torch briefly. Argyle gasped.

The two men then dragged a bewildered Argyle back to the chair.

He couldn't speak. He looked as if he was in a trance.

Domino said, 'It's cold. Close the window.'

Memoré lowered it.

Argyle was shaking his head in disbelief.

Memoré smiled. It looked as if he'd drunk three fingers of vinegar.

Domino glared at Argyle and said, 'You're next if you don't tell us where that frigging Rosary is.'

Bromersley Police Station, South Yorkshire.
Thursday, 8 December 2011. 8.28 a.m.

Detective Inspector Angel arrived in his office full of charm, cheerfulness and general goodwill to all mankind. Christmas was coming, and peace reigned supreme at home as well as at work. The previous day, he had put the final touches to his evidence in the case of the mystery of the Cheshire Cat Murders and pushed that along to Mr Twelvetrees, the barrister at the CPS, and he now had the opportunity to clear the backlog of circulars, police reports, inconsequential letters and junk emails as well as consequential letters and important emails that were on a pile in the middle of his desk. He sat down determined to reduce it. He was pulling the pile towards him when the phone rang. He glared at it then reached out and picked it up. 'Angel,' he said.

It was the duty sergeant. 'DS Clifton, sir. Last night's report, sir. I don't suppose you've had time to read it.'

'No, Bernie, I haven't. Something special on it? Tell me.'

'Got a triple nine just before midnight, sir,' he said. 'A man called Wiseman staying at the old King George Hotel reported seeing a dead body in the area at the back of the hotel. A patrol car team were sent, Sean Donohue and Cyril Elders. They said that they had a good look at the spot where the man said he saw it, but there were no signs of a body. The caller, however, Mr Wiseman, insisted that he wasn't seeing things and that he *had* seen it. He wasn't under the influence and he seemed genuine enough.'

Angel frowned and rubbed his chin.

Clifton said. 'Of course, it'll come up in *their* reports, but I thought you'd like notice of it.'

Angel pursed his lips. 'Yes,' he said. 'The lads gone off?'

'Sean Donohue is still here. Shall I send him down?'

Angel's eyebrows shot up. 'Yes, please, Bernie. Out of interest, anything else?'

'A gown shop broken into, that new posh one, Madam Vera's. Small amount of stuff taken.'

'Aye. The one with the big price tickets. Any witnesses or CCTV?'

'No, sir. And there was Ben Hill, the butcher, had a bucket stolen.'

'A bucket? What's a bucket worth, a couple of quid, a fiver?'

Clifton grinned. 'Sixty-eight quid, sir. It was a special butcher's bucket, I understand. Stainless steel and all that.'

Angel sniffed. 'About what he charges for two chops, my wife tells me. All right, Bernie, I'll pick that up when the reports come in.'

He thanked the sergeant and closed the phone.

Two minutes later Patrolman Sean Donohue knocked on the door.

'Come in, Sean. Sit down. Tell me about the triple nine.'

'It was just before midnight, we got the call from the operations room, sir. We were notified that a Mr Wiseman had reported a dead female in the car park at the back of the old King George Hotel. It's not very nice round there, sir. It's like a big backyard. Room for a few cars to park. And the pub's rubbish bins near the door to the kitchen. Anyway, me and Cyril had a good look round, but couldn't see anything. We went round to the front. The hotel entrance was closed, but the main door to the bar was still open. We had to go in there to raise anybody. The barman directed us to Wiseman's room. He was insistent that he had seen a body. He came down and showed us the place where he said he'd seen it, and was as amazed as we were that there was nothing there.'

The phone rang. Angel reached out for it.

'It's Sergeant Clifton again, sir. That witness, Mr Wiseman, is here. He's asking to see whoever's in charge. He's a bit steamed up about waiting so long for someone to contact him. Will you see him, or shall I get one of the lads to deal with him?'

Angel rubbed his chin. Wiseman sounded like a time-waster, but he couldn't be certain. Angel was used to all sorts of cranks turning up at the station under some pretext or other. He was determined to make short shrift of him if he was a time-waster.

'I had better see him, Bernie. Have somebody bring him down to my office, please,' he said and closed the phone.

Angel turned back to Sean Donohue. 'Wiseman is on his way down. Is there anything else I need to know?'

'Not really, sir. We didn't know what to do. We asked in the bar if anybody had seen anything unusual that night and nobody had. All the other rooms in the hotel had their lights out and therefore seemed to have settled down for the night. We had another look round the back just in case . . . then reported back in to Sergeant Clifton. He said leave it, but put in a full report in the morning, which I have done. And we carried on with our patrol.'

'Right, lad,' Angel said. 'Go on home and get some kip.'

'Yes, sir,' he said and out he went.

It was only a few moments later that Mr Wiseman was shown into Angel's office by a PC. The witness was sun-tanned, about 60, in a smart suit, white shirt and tie. But he didn't seem happy.

'Please sit down, sir,' Angel said. 'I believe you want to see me about the triple-nine call you made last night?'

'At last, somebody is taking some notice,' he said with a sniff. 'I don't think you are treating this murder with the urgency it clearly deserves.'

Angel blinked. 'I am sorry that you think that, sir. But we are extremely busy. This is a small town and there were more than four incidents overnight, last night, to my knowledge, needing urgent investigation, and it is impossible to deal with them all at the same time. And if my constables had seen any trace of a body — as you had reported — believe me, the matter would have received a very much greater priority.'

Wiseman's attitude didn't change. 'I think that your men think that I am stupid or mental or something, but I will tell you what happened and hope that I may convince *you* that I am sound in both mind and limb. I am a Captain in the Royal Engineers. I am near retirement and married so I am looking for a house for us to retire to around here. I am staying at the King George Hotel. It's not much of a place, but the Feathers was fully booked. Last night I went to bed about 9.30 and went to sleep almost straightaway. At around midnight . . . I'm not sure to five minutes or so, I woke up. I had to go to the bathroom. Came back. I thought the room was a bit stuffy, so I opened the window. It was very cold, but there was no wind. I looked out. I couldn't see much. My room hasn't a view. It is on the first floor, and it looks out over the back of the hotel where my car was parked. I could just make out the skyline beside the roof of the cardboard box factory. Anyway, I was looking down when, at that moment, a light went on. It was only on for a second or two. And I saw this body on the ground. A woman . . . a big mop of beautiful blonde hair . . . long bare legs covered in blood. She was wearing a dark coat or dress. And obviously dead . . . and there she was . . . blood all over . . . it was awful.'

'Where did the light come from?'

'That's it. I don't know. It all happened so quickly.'

'Was it headlights from a car?'

'I don't think so. And it was not the car-park light. I checked that with the barman. He said that light didn't work. It needed a new lamp and shade. It's not been working for years.'

'What did you do then?'

'I rang 999, then I got washed and dressed. Then your two patrolmen came up to my room. I pointed out to them where I had seen the body and then went down with them to look at it. Of course, as you will now know, it wasn't there.'

Angel leaned back in the swivel chair and licked his bottom lip with the tip of his tongue.

'Well, Inspector,' the man said, 'Do *you* believe me?'

'It's an odd story, Mr Wiseman, but yes, I believe you.'

'Good. I can't understand who moved the body and where it was moved to.'

Angel said, 'And why move the body at all? Why hang about the scene? Why didn't the murderer leave the body and make good his escape?'

Angel nipped the lobe of his ear between his finger and thumb and rubbed it several times. 'How much time elapsed between you seeing the body from your bedroom window and discovering it was no longer there?'

'About ten or fifteen minutes, I suppose.'

Angel nodded. 'That's long enough,' he said. 'I don't suppose you saw or heard any persons or traffic in the car park.'

'I was busy getting washed and dressed, Inspector. I didn't notice.'

Angel stood up. He reached out for the phone and tapped in a number. While he waited for the phone to be answered, he turned to the man and said, 'I won't detain you long, Mr Wiseman, but I would like you to return to the George and show me exactly where the body had been, also you can point out your bedroom window to me, if that's convenient to you.'

'Certainly, Inspector. I'll push on ahead and meet you in the car park,' he said.

'Thank you,' Angel said.

The phone was answered. It was DS Don Taylor, the Scene of Crimes Officer.

'Don, I want you to join me at the rear of the King George Hotel straightaway,' Angel said. 'A body was reported there, but then, apparently, went missing.'

THREE

Angel, Taylor and Wiseman arrived at the small car park at the back of the hotel within a minute of each other. There were only two other cars parked there.

Wiseman showed the two policemen the place just below his bedroom window where he said that he had seen the body, and Angel promptly instructed Taylor to scrutinize the entire area for any corroborative traces, and then asked Wiseman to show him his room.

Taylor put down kneeling pads and closely looked at the car-park surface inch by inch. He soon found three small brown spots that had dried into flakes. He thought that they might be blood, and he managed to retrieve them onto clear adhesive tape. If they were blood, it might be possible to extract the DNA and identify the owner of it. He could detect nothing else. Close by were eight large rubbish bins on wheels, usually a great source of valuable information. He lifted the lids and was surprised to find that they were all empty. He lowered the lids and continued to make a careful search of the rest of the area.

Meanwhile, Wiseman took Angel by the rickety lift up to his room on the first floor, where he showed him the bedroom window from where he said he saw the horrific sight below him on the car park. Angel looked down out of the window and reckoned that Wiseman must have been about 9 metres from the spot.

He rubbed his chin.

'What do you think, Inspector?' Wiseman said.

Angel shrugged. 'We shall carry on with our inquiries and try to get an explanation.'

Wiseman nodded. 'Thank you for taking me seriously, Inspector. You'll let me know if I can help any further with your inquiries, won't you?'

'Indeed I will. Thank you very much for your help, and good luck with your house-hunting.'

He came out of Wiseman's room, went down in the lift to the reception office and knocked on the door. He made himself known and said, 'Can I see the hotel manager, please?'

'I'm Mrs Fortescue,' the lady in the office said. 'Irene Fortescue. I'm the manager. How can I help you?'

'Can you tell me who are in the rooms on the floors above Mr Wiseman?'

She looked in a big book on the desk.

'Mr Domino of London was on the fifth floor and a Mr Memoré on the fourth. They booked in together. Mr Domino had the penthouse. He paid cash in advance for two nights.'

'Did they come by car?'

'They came in the same car driven by another man.'

'Do you have the car number?'

'I'm sorry.'

'Are they still in their rooms?'

'No. They must have left very early this morning. They didn't have breakfast.'

Angel wrinkled his nose. 'Did they say why they wanted rooms on higher floors and different floors?'

'They both said — well, Mr Domino said, that they needed quietness. He did all the talking, well, what bit of talking there was. I think the short gentleman was foreign. He rarely spoke.'

'Do you have addresses for them?'

'Oh yes,' she said and she swivelled the book round for Angel to see. He copied the addresses onto the back of an envelope from his inside pocket. 'Thank you very much, Mrs Fortescue.'

'Is there anything else, Inspector?' she said.

'Yes. I would like to have a look at their rooms.'

'Yes, of course,' she said. 'I'll get the pass key and show you up. Have they done something wrong, Inspector? Are the police looking for them?'

Angel gave her a potted version of what had been reported. 'The dead woman was described as very attractive, about thirty-five, big head of blonde hair, wearing a black dress and black coat.'

Mrs Fortescue's mouth dropped open. 'Good heavens. You won't believe it, Inspector, but a woman exactly fitting that description was in this office about half an hour ago.'

Angel blinked. 'What did she want?' he said.

'She was asking if Mr Domino was still here.'

He shook his head. It didn't make sense. 'What did she actually say?'

'I can't remember the exact words . . . she had a dreamy expression as if she was half-asleep or something. Very strange. She was quite eerie. Anyway, I rang his room, but there was no reply,' she continued. 'And when I looked round to tell her, she had gone. Disappeared into thin air. I went up to the room and knocked on the door. There was no reply so I let myself in and sure enough, he had gone.'

Angel took a moment or two to try to make sense of the puzzle. The obvious explanation was that there were two women who looked similar, were dressed similarly and had reasons for being at the hotel within a few hours of each other, and that one of them might be dead. Put like that it sounded very unlikely.

He rubbed his chin.

'I understand the outside light for the area at the rear of the hotel is not working,' he said. 'Is that correct?'

'I am afraid that the children round here use it as a target for throwing stones. It has been replaced several times and the directors decided that it would not be replaced again. I hope we are not breaking any laws?'

He shook his head. 'Not as far as I am aware.'

At that moment, there was a loud knock on the office door and a woman in a blue overall burst in. She ignored Angel and went straight up to Mrs Fortescue at her desk.

'You'll never believe it, Mrs Fortescue,' she said. 'I went to move that sofa in the penthouse suite to vacuum underneath it and it wouldn't budge. I thought it was me that was getting too old to shove it, but no. It wouldn't budge. So I went down on my knees and I could see metal pieces with big screws going through the carpet into the floorboards and the other side screwed into the legs of the sofa. Those metal fastenings are on all six legs. And they're covered with fringe so that you can't see a thing. What would anybody want to do that for? It's a sofa, it's not going to go anywhere. And nobody would want to steal it. It's not worth anything. I wouldn't give it house room. Anyway, it can't be moved. So underneath will have to stay mucky.'

Mrs Fortescue frowned.

Angel frowned.

'Leave it with me, Clarice,' Mrs Fortescue said. 'I'll go up and have a look at it for myself. Leave it for now. Finish off the corridors and the stairs.'

'Righto,' the cleaning lady said. She glanced back at Angel, then muttered, 'You never know what you're going to find next, do you?'

She went out of the office. Angel watched her leave.

Angel and Mrs Fortescue went up in the lift to the fifth floor. She let Angel into the room with her pass key. They crossed to the sofa by the window. Angel crouched down, lifted the fringe around the feet and saw the L-shaped brackets exactly as the cleaning lady had described. Then he stood up, walked round to the back of the sofa and looked at the back feet. They were secured to the floorboards in exactly the same way.

Angel crouched down and gave the sofa a mighty push. But it didn't budge.

He turned to Mrs Fortescue and said, 'Is it usually in this position?'

'No,' she said. 'It should be across the foot of the bed. I can't imagine why it has been moved. And why would anybody want to screw it down like this? I see all sorts of things in this business, but this is the wackiest I've ever come across.'

'Well, leave it where it is for now. Don't touch anything. I'll get our SOCO team to check it out.'

They went out of the room. He closed the door, and as she locked it, she said, 'Do you think there's something hidden under the sofa, Inspector?'

'I don't know,' he said, making for the lift. 'I'll get SOCO to unscrew it and take a look. Now I must see the room Mr Memoré occupied.'

She pressed the button for the fourth floor. 'I shall send a bill on to Mr Domino for damage to the carpets and for screwing holes into the furniture,' she said. 'It's disgraceful behaviour in a respectable hotel.'

Angel licked his bottom lip with the tip of his tongue thoughtfully as the lift rattled down. He was thinking that the address that gentleman had given was most likely false.

Mrs Fortescue said, 'What is it about people staying in hotels? They wouldn't behave like that in their own homes.'

They arrived at the room recently occupied by Mr Memoré.

Angel peered inside from the doorway. He noted that the bed had not been made. 'Good,' he said. Then he turned to Mrs Fortescue and said, 'This has not yet been cleaned by your staff? Please keep everybody out until our forensic team have been over it.'

Angel returned to the station. It was four o'clock and it was getting darker and colder. As he walked thoughtfully down the green corridor towards his own tiny office, he passed the open door of the CID office. He stopped, came back and looked in. Unusually, there was only one person in there. It was DC Ahmed Ahaz. He was seated at his computer screen, updating the station website. He was the youngest member of Angel's team, and was always willing and enthusiastic. Angel liked him and could see a great future for him in the force.

'Ahmed,' Angel said. 'Come into my office a minute.'

Ahmed picked up a newspaper and followed him down the corridor.

'I want you to check out two characters, Charles Domino and Joseph Memoré,' Angel said, hanging his overcoat on the hook at the side of the green stationery cupboard. 'See what you can find out.'

Angel took the envelope out from his inside jacket pocket and pointed to the note he had made. 'There are their addresses, in London.'

'Right, sir,' Ahmed said as he carefully copied the information into his notebook. As he finished, he said, 'Have you seen this morning's newspaper, sir?'

'Haven't had time for anything, lad,' he said, pointing to the pile of paperwork on his desk. 'What is it?'

Ahmed unfolded the paper he had been carrying and handed it to him. 'A big robbery in Hatton Garden, sir,' he said.

Angel sighed. 'I saw it on the telly, last night. Diamond-and-ruby Rosary belonging to Bloody Mary.'

'But did you know about *that*, sir?' Ahmed said, pointing to the bottom of the big front-page piece. 'The last sentence, sir.'

Angel took it and read it. '"Sources close to the police believe the robbers may have escaped with the Rosary to South Yorkshire."'

'So it might turn up here,' Ahmed said with a smile.

Angel frowned then shrugged. 'It might,' he said as he handed the paper back.

'Thank you, lad,' he added.

Ahmed went out.

The phone rang.

Angel reached out for it. It was DS Taylor. 'I'm speaking from the King George Hotel, sir. I thought you'd want to know. I've done the LMG test on a spec from one of the brown flakes recovered from the car park and I can confirm that it *is* blood.'

Angel's eyebrows went up. 'Right, thank you, Don. Strange thing. The blonde woman reported by Mr Wiseman to be seen dead in the car park last night was also seen this morning by Mrs Fortescue, the hotel manager, and she says she was very much alive and well.'

Taylor didn't reply immediately. 'Well, maybe there were *two* slim, identical blondes running around Bromersley?' he said.

Angel sighed. 'Yeah, and maybe they are both called Marilyn Monroe,' he said. 'No, Don, I don't think so. If just one blonde answering Wiseman's description was reported missing, then we might be able to make sense of it. In the meantime, send that specimen off to Wetherby and let's see if they have her DNA on file.'

'Right, sir.'

'Did you find anything in the rubbish bins?'

'No, sir. Believe it or not. The bins were emptied at around eight o'clock this morning.'

Angel sighed. He ran his hand across his chin.

'Not having much luck, sir,' Taylor said.

'No. How much longer are you going to be at the King George?'

'Not sure, sir. We are applying a full search and swabbing routine to the room on the fourth floor and that's well on its way. The so-called penthouse suite has been partly contaminated by the activities of the hotel cleaner, so that has very much reduced our workload there.'

'Have you unscrewed the sofa from the floor?'

'Yes, sir. And there's nothing underneath but dust,' Taylor said.

Angel pursed his lips. 'Have you lifted the floorboards?'

'We took them up. They hadn't been disturbed for a century, I bet. And there was nothing under there besides more dust.'

Angel rubbed his cheek hard. 'Have you any idea at all why the thing was screwed down in that position then, lad?'

'No, sir. Haven't a clue.'

It was 8.28 a.m., the morning of Friday, 9 December. There had been a hard frost overnight and arctic winds were gusting round the ginnels and alleyways of Bromersley.

Angel was coming down the corridor in the police station. A telephone was ringing out in the distance. As he got nearer his office, he realized that it was his own phone ringing so insistently. He wrinkled his nose, grudgingly increased his speed to the office door, pushed it open, glared at the phone, snatched it up and said, 'Angel.'

'It's Don Taylor, sir. I wondered if you were in.'

Angel's eyebrows shot up. 'Of course I'm in,' he bawled. 'I'm always in at this time, Don. I know I'm a senior officer and don't get paid by the hour, but I reckon I should at least start when the CID office opens. Anyway, what do you want, lad? It's a bit early for *you*, isn't it? Speak up.'

'It's about the two rooms at the King George Hotel, sir, in the names of Joseph Memoré and James Argyle.'

'Aye. What about them?'

'Well, sir, unusually they were both cleaned down with spirit of some sort. And there wasn't a new clear print in either room. And there was nothing in the wastepaper baskets either.'

Angel frowned and rubbed his chin. 'Real professionals, we've got, eh?' he said.

'Never before met such thoroughness, sir,' Taylor said. 'It shows they are fishy characters.'

Angel nodded. 'Right lad, thank you. By the way, you have certainly been prompt with your info. What's happening?'

'To tell the truth, sir, I've been chasing everybody round. I don't want to have to work over Christmas again.'

Angel smiled. He understood exactly. He had worked the last two Christmases and it wasn't much fun. And post-poning Christmas for a few days to fit round the investigation of a murder case might be very commendable, but it is just not the same.

'I know how you feel,' he said. He ended the call and returned the phone to its holster.

It rang immediately.

Angel snatched it up. 'Angel,' he said.

The caller inhaled noisily and then began to cough. The noise was loud and raucous. Angel instantly recognized the caller. It was his boss, Detective Superintendent Harker.

The coughing continued for twenty seconds or more. It was so loud that Angel pulled the phone away from his ear. He waited patiently. It wasn't unusual.

Eventually Harker croaked, 'Is that Angel?'

'Yes, sir,' he said.

'*There* you are. Couldn't get you.'

Harker sounded relieved, and after a further noisy intake of breath, said, 'There's been a triple nine, timed at 08:10 hours. That man Haydn King . . . boss of the brewery . . . been found dead in his swimming pool at his home on Pine Avenue . . . reported in by his butler, Meredith. I've informed SOCO and uniformed. Now this is going to be a big case, Angel. King was a very important man. And I shall want to know *every* detail of this. Report in as soon as you have the facts.'

'Right, sir,' Angel said. 'Pine Avenue? Is that the same Pine Avenue off Creesforth Road, where *you* live, sir?'

Harker coughed lightly, then said, 'Well, yes, it is. Strange, I only met the man the night before last.'

'Right, sir,' Angel said. He cancelled the call and tapped in a number.

As he waited for the phone to be answered, he couldn't help but think about the peculiarities of this life. Two men living opposite each other for more than ten years, had spoken to each other for the first time only two nights earlier, and now one of them was responsible for investigating the other's death.

He pursed his lips.

Some people might say, 'What a coincidence!'

But Angel didn't believe in coincidence.

Ahmed answered the phone. 'Yes, sir?'

Angel said: 'I am going to investigate the death of Haydn King on Pine Avenue. Find DS Crisp and DS Carter and ask them to join me there ASAP.'

FOUR

Five minutes later, Angel drove his BMW through the wrought-iron gates into the grounds of the mansion of the late Haydn King. As he swerved round the bend in the drive and passed the screen of lime trees he saw the white SOCO van, a police patrol car, Dr Mac's car and a large white Mercedes coupé. The vehicles were in a line in front of the big house. Angel parked behind them, got out of the car, locked it and made his way to the front door. A constable was on the front step stamping his feet and blowing into his hands. As he approached, the man threw up a salute.

Angel responded, then said, 'Good morning, lad. Who is in charge?'

'DS Taylor, sir. But Dr Mac, the pathologist, is here.'

'And where are they?'

'In the room where the swimming pool is, sir. That's the door facing you at the far end of the hall.'

Angel nodded, pointed his thumb at the line of cars and said, 'And who owns the white Merc?'

'Mr King's nephew. His name is Fleming, sir.'

The constable opened the door for him.

'Thanks lad,' Angel said.

As it closed behind him, he immediately felt the warmth of the house on his cheeks and the back of his hands. He glanced at the large paintings on the walls as he made his way down the long corridor on the parquet floor to the door at the end. He opened it and was immediately inside the clammy swimming pool area. The big tiled-and-glass building was bustling with SOCO men and women in white overalls, boots and masks.

He waited there and took in the scene.

DS Taylor and Dr Mac were in front of six cubicles at the end of the pool, on their knees leaning over the body of a big man with a beard in swimming trunks; his corpse lay on a white polythene sheet.

The rest of the SOCO team were engaged in taking samples of the pool water, carefully recording the temperature readings of it, and searching for fingerprints and footprints. One man was on the high diving platform with a camera, his flash tiresomely catching the attention of Angel's eye from time to time.

DS Taylor looked up from Haydn King's body, saw Angel and crossed to the door.

'Have you finished round here, Don?' Angel said, not wanting to trespass in an area not already scanned by his team.

'We've finished everything at this end, sir, around the edge of the pool, the shower and the changing cubicles,' he said, pointing out the area with a hand.

Angel's nose twitched as he observed how the muggy pool room annoyingly accentuated and echoed every syllable Taylor had uttered.

'I'll have a word with Mac,' Angel said, then he wandered to the side of the pool where the doctor was working. Taylor followed.

Angel looked down at the body, then at the doctor. 'Morning, Mac,' he said. 'What you got?'

The little Glaswegian looked up and said, 'Ah, Michael. It's a good morning for us, but not for this poor laddie. Looks like an early-morning dive that didn't go right.'

'Accidental death?'

'It's looking like that. He has a serious injury to his skull consistent with hitting his head on the edge of the pool, followed by drowning . . . but that's only what it *looks* like.'

'Do you suspect foul play, Mac?'

'I'll let you have the full SP when I've had him on the table. Might be able to phone you this afternoon.'

'That would be good. Thanks, Mac,' Angel said. Then he saw the doctor take four body-surface thermometers out of his white bag and set them on various parts of King's body. 'Time of death?' Angel said.

'I'm just working on that, Michael.'

Angel nodded. He could see that he was. He turned to Taylor. 'What you got, Don?'

'No prints round the pool area, sir. But on the curtain across the entrance to the cubicle, some smudged prints, probably the dead man's.'

Angel shook his head. 'Anything for me to work on?'

'We found him floating face down in the middle of the pool. He seems to have been in bed, taken it into his head to have a swim, and put on his trunks, dressing-gown and slippers. He came downstairs, put his gown on a coat hanger and his slippers on the shelf in that cubicle, climbed up to one of the diving boards, launched himself from there, hit the side or the bottom and died in the pool.'

Angel frowned. 'I want the pool water filtering. You'll need to organize it with the staff. Have them knock off the heating, then put filters across the drain exits and then the valves. When the pool is drained, the bottom will need close inspection.'

'Right sir,' Taylor said. 'Are you looking for anything in particular?'

'Just being thorough, lad, that's all.'

Taylor nodded. He rubbed his chin, looked down at the body and then back at Angel and said, 'I wonder if there was any reason for him to have taken his own life, sir?'

Angel said: 'I don't think I'd bother putting my dressing-gown on a coat hanger or keeping my slippers dry if I was about to commit suicide.'

Taylor wished he had thought more carefully before he had put the question.

'No, sir,' he said in a small voice.

Angel pointed to the glass-panelled doors that looked out onto a long stretch of white frosted lawn bordered with trees and evergreen bushes. 'I suppose you can access this room from the garden?'

'Yes, sir. But there are no fresh fingerprints or footprints on either side of the doors.'

Angel crossed the edge of the pool to the door. He turned the knob. It didn't give. It seemed secure. 'You found the door locked?'

'Yes, sir.'

He moved on. 'When you sweep Haydn King's bedroom, Don,' he said, 'be particularly thorough about fingerprints. I know you always are, but if there is any foul play in connection with this death, and as there's precious little here at the scene, there might be something in the bedroom.'

'Yes, sir.'

'Good,' Angel said. Then he looked behind at the cubicles and pointed at them. 'Which one did the dead man use?'

'The end one, sir,' Taylor said. 'That was where the smudged prints on the curtain were found, also the dead man's dressing-gown and slippers.'

Angel nodded. 'No clear footprints or fingerprints, I suppose?' he said.

'Everything's too wet, sir.'

Angel nodded again. He knew that Taylor was almost certain to say that, but he had hoped there might have been more prints of some sort despite the conditions. It had been known, where the prints had been greasy enough.

'I'll just have a look round,' Angel said.

'We haven't checked the steps up to the high diving board and the board itself, sir.'

He would avoid them. 'Right, I'll leave it with you. Ring me on my mobile if anything turns up.'

He turned away and sauntered thoughtfully round the changing cubicles. He carefully observed the dressing-gown, the pyjamas hanging on a peg, and the bedroom slippers on the bench in the first cubicle. He walked all the way round the swimming pool, looked closely at the low diving board at the far end, and then made his way to the door.

Angel came out of the swimming pool hall, walked up the long corridor and back into the entrance hall. He looked around, hoping that a member of the staff would be around, but there was nobody. He saw a door ajar and peered round it. He saw a big room comprising mostly upholstered settees and chairs. Some chairs were set around a big open log fire that looked very inviting.

Suddenly a man's voice called out, 'Hello there. Can I help you?'

Angel was taken aback. He had no idea who the owner of the voice was or where he was calling from. The voice sounded educated and friendly, nevertheless Angel withdrew.

The voice said, 'It's all right. Come in, old chap.'

Angel strode back through the doorway of the room.

A man in his thirties smartly dressed in an immaculate morning suit was seated by a wine table on which there was a tray of coffee. There was a copy of *The Financial Times* on his lap.

'Are you looking for somebody?' the man said.

'Yes I am,' he said, 'but I didn't mean to intrude. I am Detective Inspector Angel from Bromersley Police.'

'Ah yes, dear boy, I am Mr Haydn King's nephew, Vincent Fleming, and his next of kin. I am trying to recover from the shock of losing my dear uncle in such a tragic and unexpected way. You will probably be looking for me before the day is out. Please come in. Get warm. Would you care to join me for coffee?'

Angel pursed his lips. He didn't usually accept hospitality when he was on duty but it being such a punishingly cold day, he thought he would make an exception.

'That would be most welcome. Thank you.'

'Just apply your finger to that bell push by the side of the fireplace. Then choose a chair you fancy.'

As Angel sat down at the opposite side of the little table, Fleming closed the pages of *The Financial Times* and placed it on a chair nearby.

'This is a very sad day. Uncle Haydn was such a good swimmer. It has all been so unexpected. You'll no doubt be wanting to ask me questions, Inspector?'

Angel nodded. 'I certainly do, Mr Fleming,' he said, taking an old envelope out of his inside pocket on which he was to make notes. 'I am sorry to have to bother you at this time. Tell me, do you live here with your uncle?'

'No, Inspector. I live in Tunistone.'

Angel knew Tunistone well. It was a farming village about six miles to the west of Bromersley and a little way up the Pennines.

'How do you come to be here, then?'

'Meredith, my uncle's butler, phoned me early and told me what had happened so I came here straightaway. I can't get over it. I really can't.'

The butler Meredith came into the room. 'Excuse me, gentlemen,' he said. Then he looked at Fleming. 'You rang, sir?'

'Yes, Meredith,' Fleming said.

Angel looked across at the man. Meredith was, of course, the man who had found and reported the body in the pool, the very man he needed to see.

'Would you organize a cup for the Inspector?'

'Of course, sir,' Meredith said, then he turned to Angel and said, 'Good morning, sir.'

'Good morning, Mr Meredith,' Angel said. 'I would like to have a word with you when I have finished here, if you don't mind.'

'Yes, of course, sir,' he said. 'Please press the bell there by the fireplace, when you are ready.'

Meredith then left the room and returned almost straightaway with a cup and saucer on a silver salver. He placed the cup and saucer on the table, went out and closed the door.

Fleming poured the coffee and Angel took a sip. It tasted good.

'You live on your own, up there in Tunistone, Mr Fleming?'

'Yes. I live in a farmhouse sheltered by a hill. It is a bit cooler than here, but it is very pleasant. And there is nobody to fall out with.'

'So were you there on your own last night?'

Fleming raised his head slowly, stared at Angel, then very deliberately he said, 'I see, Inspector. You are looking for my alibi?'

Angel's eyebrows shot up. He realized that he had been a little obvious. 'I ask everybody, Mr Fleming. Everybody to do with the case in hand. It's a habit. If it offends, please excuse me.'

'But I thought it was without doubt a tragic accident?'

'It may well be, Mr Fleming. So you would have no objection to answering the question?'

Fleming looked him straight in the face and said, 'I live on my own, but I was here, dining with my uncle, until about nine o'clock. I left here and arrived home at about 9.30 and I remained there until I received a phone call from Meredith at a few minutes past eight this morning. I hope that satisfies you, Inspector.'

Angel nodded. 'Thank you.'

'If it is not an accident, Inspector, I should want to know about it. I cannot imagine who might want to harm Uncle Haydn. He looked like a tyrant, sometimes shouted like a tyrant, he could be abrupt and he was sometimes impatient, but there was no malice in him . . . none at all.'

'You know of nobody who would want to see him dead?'

'Nobody. Nobody at all,' Fleming said. He thought a moment then added, 'He went through a difficult divorce three years ago. His wife, Auntie Judy — she's now reverted to her maiden name, Miss Judy Savage — was a bit of a fire-cracker. They fought like cat and dog. And Uncle Haydn could be so aggravating and annoying, but there was no harm in him at all. Of course, she never thought the settlement was equitable when they split up. I don't suppose she would have thought any amount would have been enough. He may well have annoyed her, but nothing more.'

'Does she live locally?'

'Oh yes. She still lives in Bromersley.'

'I will need to speak with her, also Mr King's solicitor. Do you happen to have their names and addresses? Also, I had better have yours.'

Fleming supplied him with the information and Angel scribbled it on an envelope from out of his inside pocket. Angel thanked him and brought the interview appropriately to an end. He pressed the button by the fireplace and went into the hall.

FIVE

Meredith arrived promptly in the hall in response to the bell. He came through the door from the basement kitchen.

Angel said, 'Just a few questions, Mr Meredith?'

'Anything I can do to help, sir.'

'Is there anywhere we can go that would be private, Mr Meredith?'

'There's Mr King's little sitting room that he used occasionally to watch the television, sir. It is through here,' Meredith said, opening one of the six or seven doors leading from the long corridor off the entrance hall.

When they had settled, Angel said, 'I understand that it was you who found the body?'

'Yes, sir. I took Mr King his early-morning tea at seven o'clock, which I have done every morning for twenty years, but he was not in his bed.'

'And that was unusual?'

'Very unusual, sir. He had been complaining that he didn't sleep as well as he used to. I knew that he always had a lot on his mind with the business, and I thought that he must have some transient problem. He complained similarly during the court case with the ex-Mrs King, and indeed during his mother's illness, so I had expected it to pass in time.'

'Mr King's mother died recently?'

'She broke her leg playing tennis in July 2004, sir. But it didn't heal properly. She eventually died of heart failure in January 2005. Mr King was devoted to her. She was a delightful lady. Second cousin to the Earl of Kinross. Mr King has kept her room exactly as it was in her lifetime. He will still not permit anything of hers to be thrown away. I saw him through that. And I saw him through his divorce.'

'So there was something on his mind?'

'I fear that there was, sir.'

'He confided in you, then, Mr Meredith?'

'In some things, sir. But not everything. It was just that occasionally some mornings, especially lately, he would ask for two paracetamol tablets. When I inquired into his need for them, he would mutter that he had had a bad night and had woken with a heavy head.'

'I see.'

'About two weeks ago, he told me about a recurring nightmare that he had had which disturbed him. Apparently he was having the dream most nights. He said that he used to wake in a sweat and sometimes couldn't get back to sleep. He used to dream that he saw himself floating face downwards in the swimming pool and that he was dead.'

Angel frowned. He squeezed the lobe of one ear between finger and thumb.

Meredith said, 'Since that's how I found him this morning, sir, I find it very strange.'

'Yes, indeed,' Angel said as he continued to play with his ear. This was a very interesting and puzzling situation.

Meredith said, 'Might I ask, sir, if you are the Inspector Michael Angel who is frequently reported in the newspapers as the man who always gets his man, like the Mounties?'

The muscles of Angel's face tightened. He rubbed his chin. That sort of question always made him feel uneasy. He was always afraid that one day, he would fail to get his man.

'I suppose I am,' he said at length.

'I saw you interviewed on the television after you solved that remarkable case the media dubbed the Cheshire Cat Murders, I think it was. It was amazing how you unravelled all that business with that dreadful schoolmistress.'

Yes. Well er, thank you, Mr Meredith,' Angel said. He quickly looked down at his notes, then he said, 'Tell me, what did you do when you discovered Mr King was not in his bed?'

'I thought he might be in his bathroom, but he wasn't. I noticed that his dressing-gown and slippers were missing so I reasoned that he would be somewhere in the house. I had occasionally found him working in his study and frequently in the swimming pool. Anyway I took the tray down to the study, then I saw a light from the end of the hall; it was from the partly open door to the swimming pool, so I knew he must be in there. I went along the hall and pushed open the door and got the shock of my life. There he was, face down in the middle of the pool. He was absolutely motionless and his face was under water so I knew he must be dead. I left everything as it was, and rushed out to the hall. My heart was pounding. My mind was in turmoil. I was so shocked. I had to sit down on the hall chair. All sorts of thoughts were rushing through my head. I realized that I must pull myself together and make the call. I lifted the phone and dialled 999. The rest, sir, I believe you know.'

Angel nodded. 'It must have been awful for you, Mr Meredith.'

Meredith took out a spotless white handkerchief and wiped a moist eye.

'Did it occur to you that it might not have been an accident? That there may have been somebody else in the house?'

'No, sir. Not at all. I would have known, I believe, if there had been. I had checked all the windows and doors last thing.'

'Was Mr King's behaviour last evening in any way unusual?'

'No sir. Mr Vincent Fleming, Mr King's nephew, was a dinner guest. There were no callers, and no phone calls. I served dinner at seven and cleared the table when the gentlemen retired to Mr King's study at about 7.45. I ensured that they needed nothing else, and that was the time I checked round the windows and doors, then I retired to my own room.'

'How long have you been Mr King's butler?' Angel said.

'I've been Mr King's butler for twenty years.'

'I understand that he had been married but was now divorced. What was the reason for the divorce?'

'Mr and Mrs King were very discreet, and I am glad to say that generally, I was not present during their . . . disagreements.'

Meredith then looked up at the ceiling in an effort to illustrate further that he was a cut above the plebs, which was as well, because Angel was trying subtly to cover his mouth to conceal his smile at the word 'disagreements' which the butler seemed to have had difficulty in choosing.

Angel said, 'But you were there during some of them. Tell me, what did they argue about?'

Meredith lifted his head again and said, 'This is rather distasteful for me, sir. People in my kind of employment are bound by an unwritten law that whatever we see or hear in the course of our duties is confidential and should not be repeated.'

Angel pursed his lips. 'I know exactly what you mean, Mr Meredith. The police are bound by a similar law except that in our case, it is written down and published.'

The butler just looked at him.

Angel said, 'Very well, I will not pursue it.'

Meredith seemed to relax back into the chair.

Then Angel said, 'Perhaps Miss Savage will want to speak to me about that.'

Meredith's eyes flashed. His pupils darted in different directions, but he quickly recovered. He lowered his eyebrows.

Angel pretended not to notice. He pursed his lips and squeezed the lobe of his ear between finger and thumb again. And waited.

Meredith said, 'I take your point, sir.' He took a deep breath and said, 'The point of contention, as far as I could see, was generally the amount Mrs King — as she was then — spent. This came to a climax when the bills for refurbishing their house in Florida began to come in.'

Angel nodded. 'Did either Mr or Mrs King have a relationship with some other person, as far as you know?'

'Oh no, sir. There was nothing like that. I would say simply that they were, very unfortunately, badly mismatched. They seemed not to be able to agree about anything. Mrs King even objected to the presence of Mr Fleming — Mr King's only nephew — at the family's Christmas luncheon party.'

'On what grounds?'

'She didn't like him, sir. I remember she once described him — if you will excuse me, sir — as being "too smooth".'

Angel nodded. 'Who else works here in the house?'

'I am the only member of staff who lives in, sir. Then there are Mrs Johnson, the cook housekeeper, Mr Saw, Mr King's private secretary and Mr Rogers his chauffeur, who all live locally.'

'So did you see Mr Fleming out of the house last night?'

'No, sir. He saw himself out. He usually does. He has his own front door key.'

'And how many keys are there?'

'The back-door key is left in the lock, sir. I unlock it in the morning and lock it at night. Apart from Mr King, Mr Fleming and myself, Mrs Johnson and Mr Saw have front door keys.'

'That's five keyholders, Mr Meredith? I think that's about it for now. Before I take a look at the bedroom, I would like to ask if you have any thoughts on how Mr King finished up like that . . . in the swimming pool?'

Meredith looked down at the carpet, shook his head and said, 'I've really no idea, sir.'

'I was wondering if he had recently experienced a change in circumstances of some sort . . . received some bad news concerning his health or the business? You worked for him for twenty years, had he become preoccupied over the past few days or weeks? You know, did be behave uncharacteristically?'

'He was perhaps slower in his replies of late, sir. I often had to repeat what I had said. Also he seemed not to be able to make decisions promptly — not even in small things. I suppose they might be as a result of the nightmares he was having.'

Angel rubbed his chin. 'Right,' he said.

Then Meredith's face suddenly brightened. He lifted a finger and said, 'Do you know, sir, I have just had a thought. It is all very strange. I know that Mr King asked your Superintendent Harker to visit him two nights ago. *He* was from Bromersley Police. You probably know him. I have no idea what the meeting was about. Perhaps your superintendent may be able to throw some light on what was troubling him.'

'Of course,' Angel said. 'I'll be certain to ask him.'

'I fear they didn't part on good terms, sir,' Meredith said.

Angel was not a bit surprised. He controlled a smirk. He put the envelope on which he had been making notes back into his pocket, stood up and said, 'Now then, will you show me the rest of the house?'

'Certainly, sir,' Meredith said, also getting to his feet.

Angel's mobile rang out. He reached into his pocket. The caller was Don Taylor.

'Are you free to talk, sir?'

'I'm with Mr King's butler, Mr Meredith, Don. If you can make it quick . . . ?'

'Er right. I'm still in the swimming pool room, sir,' he said. 'I thought you would want to know urgently that we've been all round the edge of the pool and the diving boards twice with a mixture of LMG and hydrogen peroxide. And we could not find any mark or trace of a recent impact with Haydn King's head or anything else human. Not even a hair.'

Angel's eyes narrowed. He slumped back down in the chair. Taylor was saying that the severe head injury was *not* received by the dead man as the result of a careless or accidental dive or fall into the pool. So Haydn King must have therefore incurred the head wound *before* his body hit the water.

Angel sighed. That information made the situation look black. It was now almost certainly murder. Mac would throw decisive light onto the case when he had concluded the post-mortem.

'I've got your point, Don,' Angel said. 'And thank you. You'd better tape up King's bedroom, bathroom and study ASAP until you can get to them. I don't want any evidence in those rooms contaminating.'

'Right, sir, straightaway. By the by, Flora has arrived and she's looking for you.'

'Send her up. I'm in a little room off the main hall.'

Angel closed the phone and turned back to the butler. 'We will have to postpone my tour of the house, Mr Meredith. The forensic team need to look in some of the rooms and we must, therefore, not contaminate them. Instead, if I may use this room, I would like to see the other members of Mr King's staff. Perhaps I could begin with Mr Saw, Mr King's secretary?'

'Of course, sir. Now if you've finished with me, I'll find him and send him to you.'

'Thank you.'

The butler made purposely for the door.

'One of my sergeants will be looking for me. Please leave the door open.'

'Right, sir,' Meredith said and he went out.

Angel leaned back in the comfortable chair and rubbed his chin as he came to terms with the fact that he probably had another murder case on his hands. Although he'd been twelve years in homicide at Bromersley, it only seemed like a couple of weeks. The sound of footsteps on the parquet flooring in the hall outside brought him back to the present.

'Is that DS Carter?' he said.

A pretty face appeared round the edge of the door. 'Yes, sir,' she said brightly.

Detective Sergeant Flora Carter had only been with Angel for two years. And she had already proved her diligence, accuracy and attention to detail. She was not married nor in a relationship and was quite the most glamorous member of the Bromersley force. Angel liked her a lot. She also smelled of aloe vera, which reminded him of holidays in Morecambe with his favourite aunt years ago.

'Come in, lass. You've been a helluva long time.'

'Sorry, sir. Got caught up with Mrs Winstone from "Vera's" gown shop in the arcade. She was making a big fuss about the broken window and the missing dresses and coats.'

The muscles round Angel's mouth tightened. 'You should have passed her on to a PC.'

'She wouldn't have liked that, sir.'

'I don't care what *she* would have liked,' he roared. 'I told Ahmed to ask you to join me promptly, and that's what I meant.'

'Yes, sir,' she said, biting her bottom lip.

'Has Don Taylor told you the about the situation here?'

'Yes, sir.'

'This is almost certainly a murder case, Flora. I want you to find Haydn King's solicitor. That chap, Meredith, the butler, will be able to give you his name and address, I expect. They should have his will. I want to know who benefits from the man's death. And I want it double quick.'

'Right, sir,' she said and made for the door.

'By the way,' he said, 'have you seen Trevor Crisp on your travels?'

Flora looked back. 'No, sir.'

He clenched his fists. 'Well, if you see him,' he said, 'tell him I want him. And I want him *now*.'

She nodded, then went out and closed the door.

He heard her running footsteps fading away down the hall followed by the slam of the front door. Seconds later there was a knock on the room door.

'Come in,' Angel called.

A stocky middle-aged man came in.

'Detective Inspector Angel?' the man said. 'I'm Harry Saw. You wanted to see me. I was Mr King's personal secretary.'

'Yes. Please sit down. I am trying to find out what happened. Have you any idea how Mr King's body came to be found dead, floating in the swimming pool?'

'No, but it's dreadful. Absolutely dreadful. I can't get over it. And it's difficult to understand. It must have been an accident. He was a very good swimmer.'

'Did he swim a lot?'

'Several times a week. For an hour or so, usually at the weekend, sometimes in the evening.'

'Did he ever mention anything about a recurring dream he was having?'

Saw's eyes narrowed. 'No,' he said.

'Can you tell me if there was anything in his family or social or business life that was troubling him?'

'That's not easy to answer, Inspector. He was divorced and didn't have any children, so he didn't have a family life. He had no friends, was not a member of any association or club, so he didn't have a social life either. His sole interest was the business. He was, of course, very progressive. He liked to make things happen. So the business was always in a state of development, and inevitably, problems, questions and difficulties arose every day. But he thrived on it, and he was used to it, and he usually dealt with them effortlessly and methodically as they came along. I am not aware that there was anything particular bothering him.'

Angel nodded. 'He was a man of method?'

'Absolutely. He wrote everything important in his diary. Although he had an excellent memory, he never relied on it. Appointments, follow-up dates and so on. If someone promised to do something or have something delivered by a certain day or time, he would note it in the appointment diary. And if it wasn't kept to, whoever it was was for the high jump.'

Angel nodded. He pursed his lips. Meredith had said that he thought something *was* troubling his employer. He needed to find out more about that nightmare. He also needed to know what had passed between King and the superintendent.

'Well, thank you very much, Mr Saw. If you think of anything, please let me know.'

Harry Saw nodded. 'I certainly will.'

'Would you be kind enough to ask Mrs Johnson to see me, please?'

'I believe that she is in the kitchen. I will phone her and ask her to come up,' Saw said and he went out.

Angel leaned back the chair and began to think out the questions he needed to ask the woman.

There was a quick knock on the door, a rattle of the doorknob and the door opened. A man looked round the room. It was DS Crisp. When his eyes met Angel's, he gave him a breezy smile. 'There you are, sir,' Crisp said.

Angel's top lip tightened across his teeth.

Trevor Crisp had been on his team for six years and generally Angel considered him to be a good detective. However, he frequently disappeared for hours at a time without ever giving a satisfactory explanation. When pressed, he inevitably gave a tomfool reason that could never be proved and this was guaranteed to make Angel furious.

'Where the hell have you been?' Angel roared. 'On your holidays? Come in and close the door. You're like the Scarlet Pimpernel. I can never bloody well find you.'

'And *I've* been looking for *you*, sir.'

'All this time? Well, I assure you, I have not been playing "Hide and Seek". I told Ahmed to ask you to meet me here more than an hour ago. Didn't you get the message?'

'I got caught up with Ben Hill, the butcher. He had—'

'I don't care who you got caught up with. And I know about his losing a bucket worth £68, if that was all it was about. You could have got a PC to deal with *that*. When I say I want you here, Crisp, I want you here, lad. Right?'

'It was difficult, sir,' Crisp said.

Angel's eyes flashed. He stood up. 'Life *is* difficult! It always will be. It's all about decisions, priorities and options.

I'm not difficult to work for, but when I ask you to do something I expect you to do it, not get diverted by a butcher bleating about a stolen bucket — or anybody else, for that matter. Now let's get on. This case is about the death of a man. It is probably murder. So I want you to get your skates on and make up for the time lost. I want to find out about Haydn King and King's Breweries plc. Firstly, find out from records if there is anything known about the dead man and let me know. Then contact the National Crime Operations Faculty at Wakefield HQ. Speak to their expert in financial matters and find out how King's Breweries are doing, whether the share is regarded as a good buy, if there are any topical stories circulating about the business, or about Haydn King, and so on. All right?'

'Right, sir,' Crisp said.

'Crack on with it then, lad!'

'Yes, sir,' Crisp said and he dashed out.

Angel sighed. He sat down and shook his head. He picked up his notes, read through them and tidied up the writing, putting loops where needed on the letters, crossing the 't's and so on to make it more legible.

There was a loud knock on the door.

'Come in,' he called.

A small woman in a white coat looked in. 'Ah yes. Is it Inspector Angel?' she said. 'You wanted to see me.'

'I do,' he said. 'And you must be Mrs Johnson. Please come in and sit down. I would like to ask you a few questions. Won't take long.'

She closed the door and strode confidently over to the chair opposite him. 'Take as long as you want, Inspector. I have very little to do, now that Mr King has passed on. I don't even know if I have a job anymore. It's dreadful. Perfectly dreadful. You never know what's coming next, do you? And Mr Meredith said he was a good swimmer. If he was that good a swimmer, you wouldn't think that such an accident could happen, would you?'

Angel rubbed his chin and frowned. 'I beg your pardon?' he said.

'Well, diving into the pool, like that, and hitting his head,' she said.

'It may not have been quite like that, Mrs Johnson. That's why I am interested in what you might be able to tell me.'

Her eyes grew as big as two fried eggs in a pan. 'I wondered why you was asking everybody so many questions. You mean it was . . . it was *murder*?' she said.

'May have been,' he said at length.

Her mouth dropped open. 'I can't tell you nuthin' about that,' she said. Then she peered at him for several seconds. 'Do you know, Inspector, you look a lot younger than them photographs they put of you in the papers.'

Angel shook his head impatiently. 'Do you know of anybody who would have wanted to murder him?'

'Oh yes,' she said. 'Just about everybody, I should think. He was the most aggravating man you could wish to meet. He had no patience and he was impossible to please. I looked after him for years. I should know.'

Angel thought for a second before he said, 'We have also to consider the possibility that Mr King might have taken his own life.'

'Not him. Not in a thousand years. He thought he was King Dick. He could never have topped himself. Oh no.'

Angel considered her answer and moved on. 'Did you see him often?'

'Every day,' she said. 'I used to cook his breakfast and serve it at 7.25 exactly. He was very particular about that. Then, just before he went to the office, he would call me in and we'd discuss the following day's menu, also he would tell me if he wanted me to do anything different about his clothes or the laundry or the way I laid a tray or the windows or whatever. He could always find something to complain about.'

'And did you find him any different these past few days?'

'No. He was just as difficult as he always was.'

'You didn't find him at all dreamy or vague, as if his thoughts were somewhere else?'

'No. I've been here for four years, and he's always been the same. Difficult, cantankerous, awkward and unreasonable. No wonder Mrs King walked out on him. I'd have hit him on the head with something if he'd been mine, I can tell you.'

'But he wasn't worse than usual or different these past few weeks or days?'

'No, Inspector. I've told you. He's always been the same miserable, nit-picking so-and-so ever since I knowed him.'

'Did he ever tell you about his dreams or nightmares?'

'Naw, he wouldn't tell me anything like that. All we ever talked about was meals, money and muck. He wasn't much with the social chat, Inspector.'

'Right, thank you, Mrs Johnson.'

'Is that all you want to know?' she said, jumping out of the chair.

'For now, thank you. Yes. Now I want to see Mr King's chauffeur . . .'

'Mark Rogers. He's outside waiting,' she said, making for the door. She looked back and added, 'And if you hear of anybody wanting a good housekeeper, tell them I will be looking for a good job in a week or two, will you?'

He hesitated. 'I doubt if I shall meet anybody that could afford you,' he said.

She frowned. It turned to a smile as she pulled open the door. 'You're right there, Inspector,' she chuckled.

Angel added, 'Ask Mr Rogers to come in, will you?'

'Very well, Inspector.'

SIX

There was a knock at the door and it was opened by a smart young man in his thirties. He wore a dark suit and carried a peaked hat.

He closed the door and turned to face Angel.

'Please come in and sit down,' Angel said.

The young man came tentatively into the small sitting room and sat down in a chair opposite Angel.

'You were Mr King's chauffeur?'

'Yes, sir,' he said. 'Mark Rogers. I also maintained his cars.'

'How long have you worked for Mr King?'

'It's about eight years now.'

'And what exactly did you do? What did you do yesterday, for instance?'

'Hmm. Yesterday? Well, I picked him up in the Mercedes at eight o'clock and took him to the Head Office on Pontefract Road, then I came back here. I was getting some warm water to wash the upholstery when my mobile rang. It was a message to say that Mr King wanted me back there straightaway to take him to Blackburn. The company has a brewery there. So I put my best jacket back on and my hat and dashed back to Pontefract Road to pick him up. He wasn't pleased because I'd kept him waiting three minutes. He took a secretary with him and dictated some emails to her. He also made some phone calls. Anyway, I got them there for eleven. He said he wouldn't be long, but it was actually after two before they returned. It was a good job I had my sandwiches because it was after four before I got back to Pontefract Road. I dropped them off and then filled up the car with diesel. I returned to Pontefract Road and waited until 5.30 when I brought Mr King back here, then I knocked off and went home.'

'Have you any idea how he came to be found dead in the swimming pool?'

'No, sir. None at all.'

'Did you notice any difference in his manner this last week or so?'

'No, sir. There was one thing about Mr King, and that was he was always the same. He never seemed to vary. He told me what to do, and as long as I did it, he was satisfied. He never grumbled as long as he got his own way. If he wanted to go somewhere, I took him there the quickest and safest way I knew. He was a bit short on charm and was never polite, but I could live with that. He was the boss, he paid my wages, good wages, and he didn't mess about. That satisfied me.'

'So you never noticed that he was worried or afraid or nervous about anything lately, as if he had something on his mind?'

Rogers' eyebrows shot up. 'Mr King? No, sir. The only thing he was bothered about was the business. As long as the breweries kept on making the booze and selling it, nothing else seemed to bother him.'

'Did he ever tell you about the dreams he was having?'

'Dreams? No. I would have thought he would have been far too busy to have time for dreams, sir.'

'And you saw no change in him at all this past week or so?'

'No, sir. Not at all. The only time I've seen him the slightest bit out of sorts was when he and his wife were having their bits of trouble a few years back. But even then he wasn't miserable. He was just angry, wild with anger. It was a difficult time for everybody, I can tell you. I was glad when they separated and finally got divorced.'

Angel rubbed his chin. 'He was found this morning dead in the swimming pool. Have you any idea how this might have happened?'

'No idea. Why should I know anything about that?'

'Just asking. And you didn't notice any change in him over the past week or so, any forgetfulness and so on, as if he had something on his mind . . . something troubling him?'

'No, sir. As I have said, he was the same as always. The one good thing you could say about the boss in the years I worked for him was that he was consistent. Do what he wanted and there was peace, cross him and he'd cuss you from here to hell and back.'

Angel nodded. 'Right, Mr Rogers. Thank you very much.'

Angel stopped the BMW outside the white-painted hacienda-style house on Creesforth Road, Bromersley; it was clearly a one-off, architect-designed house. He got out of the car and locked it. He opened the big, wooden gate and went into the front yard, past the pampas grass, round the fountain and up the six steps to the dome-topped door. He pressed the bell push and waited.

The door was eventually opened slowly by a pretty girl of about seventeen.

He smiled. She smiled back.

'Could I see Miss Judy Savage, please?' he said. He produced a card from his top pocket and offered it to her.

From inside the house a raucous female voice like a hellcat yelled out, 'What is it?'

The girl gasped, took the card and ran inside, leaving the door wide open.

Angel peered down the wood-panelled hall and the highly polished wooden floor. He heard the two female voices chattering briefly, then a strikingly tall woman in a white turban and a multi-coloured kaftan, holding a long-handled paintbrush in one hand and his card in the other, appeared framed in an open doorway at the other end of the hall. She looked across at him. She seemed to like what she saw. She smiled.

Angel stared back. He noted the figure, the shapely hips, the long legs, the tiny waist and the bosom to suckle for Yorkshire. She had a face that could sell a shipload of beauty cream, with cheekbones higher than Strangeways clocktower.

He pursed his lips. She must be Judy Savage.

He couldn't take his eyes off her.

'Come in, Inspector. Don't stand on the doorstep getting cold,' she said, in a voice as sweet as a girl experiencing her first shot of cocaine. 'Please excuse my maid. She isn't used to er . . . answering the door to handsome young men.'

He hesitated. He must be wary. He moistened his bottom lip with the tip of his tongue.

She smiled broadly. 'Will you follow me?' she said, turning, and led him through an arch and along a corridor.

Angel sailed along behind in a slipstream of perfume.

'I'm taking you down to my studio. I am working at something very particular and I don't want to leave it until it is finished. I can't think what you want, Inspector. I don't mean that you are not welcome, but I don't owe anybody anything. I paid that speeding fine ages ago.'

'It's not about a speeding fine.'

'I told the man I'd get a TV licence when I get a new cheque book. The service at my bank is dreadful.'

They passed several doors and reached a large, airy room at the end. She floated in first and he followed her. When he looked round the room, his mouth dropped open. The walls were covered with brightly coloured paintings of every subject you could think of: pastoral scenes, ships, city buildings, children at play, portraits, naked men and women, and geometric shapes.

On many of the paintings there was an arrow pointing at some feature followed by a roughly daubed sentence.

One pointed at a man with no clothes and read, 'Shivering because he is too poor to buy clothes.' On another, a painting of a crowded city centre consisting of high-rise buildings, an arrow was pointed at one of the buildings and read, 'Used to be a hospital, now offices for United International Oil.' Some of the paintings had groups of tiny silver stars printed on paper stuck around the head of a character on top of the canvas or paper.

A sofa in the corner was loaded with more canvases. There was an easel standing in another corner, and three dining chairs around a big table in the centre of the room. It was cluttered with pots and tubes of paint, jam jars and milk bottles with brushes sticking out of them, and a half-finished watercolour on a board.

Judy Savage noticed Angel's reaction to the canvases and smiled. 'Do you like my paintings, Inspector?'

He hesitated, then returned the smile and said, 'They're different.'

She didn't like his answer. She pouted, sat down at the table in front of the watercolour and pointed to the dining chair closest to her.

'I'm not into modern art, Miss Savage,' Angel said, pulling out the chair. 'My opinion isn't worth a . . . isn't worth anything.'

She turned on a bewitching smile. 'They're very highly thought of in New York and Boston,' she said. 'That's the United States, you know. I have a show in New York in April.'

It sounded important. Angel wondered if she was telling the truth. He would be the first to admit he knew nothing about modern culture.

She looked at him and smiled again, displaying two beautiful rows of matching teeth and a pair of pink, seductive lips. He struggled to think of a reply. It wasn't easy for him to make an honest yet kind comment about her strange collages.

He couldn't help but smile. 'I hope you have a very good show,' he said.

She smiled like an angel. 'Well, thank you,' she said.

She rattled the brush she was holding in a tall vase of dark grey water on the table, squeezed off most of the water between finger and thumb onto a duster, looked undecided down at the palette of paints, then looked up smiling and said, 'I'm not saying that it isn't nice having you here, Inspector Angel, but what exactly did you want to see me about?'

Angel rubbed his chin. 'It's about your ex-husband.'

The angelic smile was replaced by a scowl. Her face went scarlet. She stood up and banged the chair noisily on the floor. 'Oh *him*!' she screamed in the raucous voice he had heard earlier. 'What about him? He's not getting a penny back if that's what he's after. I am not afraid to go back to court if that is necessary. He needn't think I am too afraid to sit in front of a courtroom full of people.'

Angel winced. 'It's not that at all, Miss Savage,' he said. 'Nobody wants anything. Please sit down.'

She frowned. She looked round for her chair, snatched at it and sat back down at the table. She breathed in and out slowly three times, shook her head and said, 'Well, if it's not about money, what is it about, then?'

Angel took a count of three. 'The fact is that Haydn King was found dead in the swimming pool this morning,' he said.

She looked up. Her mouth dropped open. The excess colour left her face, and her big blue eyes glided gently to the left and then to the right and then back again.

She breathed out. 'Oh, I see,' she said quietly. 'Oh, dear. Oh, dear me. Must have been an accident?'

'We are not sure yet. That's why I wondered if you could assist us with our inquiries?'

'The poor dear man,' she said. 'He was the only man I ever really loved.'

Angel sat there patiently. He wanted to give her time to recover from the shock of the news.

'And we could have made a go of it, if it hadn't been for that nephew of his,' she said.

He realized she was referring to Vincent Fleming.

'I'm not sure I can help, Inspector,' she said. 'It is some time since I saw Haydn. In fact, I thought I had finished with him forever. It is three years since our divorce, and it has taken him two years after that to shell out the settlement in full.'

'Oh, well, let's see how we go,' Angel said, glad to get down to business. 'I understand that Mr King was a very good swimmer.'

'He had a cabinet full of silver cups and shields, all for swimming and diving.'

'When you knew him, was he ever depressed or in need of any emotional support?'

Her eyebrows shot up. 'Emotional support? Do you mean pills?'

'Not exclusively. It has been suggested that he was worried about something. Was he at all likely to have taken his own life?'

'Huh! No, Inspector. Not the Haydn King I knew. I never saw him like that. He said that if he was worried about something, he would go to where the trouble was and cut it out and destroy it, or pay to have somebody else do it. I think he would be the last person in the world to take his own life.'

'Was he ever at all dreamy . . . forgetful . . . as if he had something else on his mind?'

'Never. Are you still talking about Haydn King? Huh. He hadn't the time or the patience to be dreamy.'

Angel frowned. 'May I ask, Miss Savage, what the grounds were for the divorce?'

'Incompatibility. It should have been for mental cruelty, but my barrister said that that was always hard to prove. He was rotten to me. He hadn't an ounce of love in him. At least not for me. All he loved was his precious business. And that nephew, Vincent. He was the most difficult man I have ever known. And he didn't appreciate art. And *was* he mean? I had to fight for every penny of my settlement. There were times when I would happily have killed him.'

She didn't realize the significance of what she had said. Angel gave her a sideways look, but she didn't seem to notice.

He stood up. 'Well, Miss Savage, I think that's about all for now,' he said. 'Thank you very much.'

Realizing he was leaving, she also stood up. He held out his hand and shook hers very gently. He turned towards the door, then quickly turned back. 'Oh, there's just one small thing, Miss Savage.'

'Yes, Inspector?'

'Just for the record. Where did you spend last evening and overnight?'

'Why, here, of course. I was painting away. I have a collection to get together for my show in April.'

'And who was with you?'

She smiled and looked at him, with her head tilted slightly and her big eyes as shiny as the Chief Constable's buttons. She liked him. She liked his strong face, his powerful, athletic body, his even white teeth and his jet-black hair. 'Nobody was with me,' she said, coming up very close. 'I was *all* on my own. *All* night.' She ran her hand tenderly through his hair and whispered in his ear. 'Like I am now.'

If Angel had been a philanderer, he might have philandered, but he wasn't and he didn't.

It was four o'clock, the sky was dark and the temperature was below freezing when Angel arrived at the station. He went past his own office and along the corridor to the superintendent's office at the end, where he stopped and sighed as he knocked on the door.

'Come in,' Harker said.

Angel lowered the handle and went into the office.

The room was as hot as the boiler room at Strangeways, also there was a repetitive tinny clanking noise that sounded like a cat desperately trying to withdraw its head from a tin can. He looked around for the explanation and discovered that Harker had a very old fan heater on the floor by his feet.

'Sit down, lad,' Harker said from behind his desk, dodging between the heaped piles of papers, reports, circulars and boxes of Kleenex and Movicol. The superintendent's head was shaped like a turnip, Angel noticed, and his skin the colour of the walls in the lavatories in Strangeways.

Angel wrinkled his nose defensively at the distinctive smell of TCP.

'You've come to tell me about Haydn King?' Harker said.

'Yes, sir,' he said. 'Of course, I have no absolute conclusions yet, but—'

Harker cut in. 'He took his own life while the balance of his mind was disturbed.'

Angel frowned. 'No, sir. I had rejected that as a possibility. I was about to say that it seemed to be either accidental or it was murder.'

'No,' Harker said. 'I think you've got murder on the brain, lad.'

The superintendent took a stick inhaler out of his pocket, removed the cover and inserted it up a nostril. He inhaled noisily, pulled it out, waited a moment to test its efficacy, nodded approvingly, replaced the cover on the inhaler and put it back in his pocket.

He looked at Angel, sniffed and said, 'I know you think you're somebody special just because you've had a lot of luck and your name is always in the papers. But in this station, you're just an ordinary police inspector — one of thousands. So there's no reason to try to make a bigger thing out of this case than it really merits, just because the victim is a significant local businessman.'

Angel struggled to think of something to say that wasn't gratuitously rude, but he couldn't think of anything.

'I was simply saying that I had not come to any conclusion,' he said. He then went on to tell him what he had found when he arrived at the swimming pool that morning, what DS Taylor had told him about the lack of any forensic evidence on the pool tiles and diving board edges, and the essence of what King's nephew, staff and ex-wife had said in answer to his questions.

At the end of the report, Harker sniffed and rubbed his chin. 'I told you he took his own life.' Then he told Angel about being summoned to see the great man on the Tuesday evening previous and the conversation that had followed.

The further Harker's story unfolded, the deeper became Angel's frown.

When he'd finished, Angel said, 'I am afraid, sir, that your evidence is critical to the case.'

'I have already come to that conclusion, lad. And I'm not putting myself in a situation where every Tom, Dick or Harry can keep cross-questioning me, so I will make a deposition for our barrister, Twelvetrees, to submit, and I'll see that you get a copy. All right?'

Angel had no option but to agree. Then he said, 'By the way, sir, King mentioned the nightmare to his butler, but I have not yet found anybody else he told.'

'Well, it is not something he would want to have broadcast, lad,' he said. 'He wouldn't want it known that a persistent bad dream he was having had any effect on him. They might have thought that he was going soft, or in need of psychiatric treatment. You couldn't have a man in charge of thousands of jobs and millions of pounds of investors' funds being known to be affected by a dream. People might have lost confidence in him.'

'Yes, sir, but maybe he *was* in need of psychiatric attention.'

'Possibly. He behaved most aggressively to me when I said that dreams were not a matter for the police, that regretfully we were not able to assist him, and that I thought a doctor might be able to help him, also that he might benefit from a holiday.'

Angel nodded. 'I will see his doctor, sir. He may be able to throw some light on his mental state.'

'I am very sorry to hear of Mr King's death, Inspector,' Doctor Singh said, looking at his computer screen. 'By the look of it, he hasn't needed much attention from this practice. According to his record, he had a viral infection in February 2000. I attended him. Prescribed an antibiotic. No follow-up call was required, so it seemed to have cleared that up all right.'

'Is that all, Doctor?'

'No. As a matter of fact I saw him only a few days ago.'

Angel's head went up. 'When exactly?'

'December 5th.'

Angel frowned. 'That was Monday, only four days ago,' he said.

He recalled that that was the day before King summoned Harker to his house and told him about the dreams.

'Yes. He complained of severe pain in his big toe. I saw him at his office. He thought he might have sprained it, however it was simply gout. I left him with a prescription. It doesn't usually take long to clear gout these days.'

'Did he speak to you about anything else at that time, Doctor?'

'No. I'm sure that he didn't.'

Angel told him the story about the recurrent nightmare relayed to him by Meredith and Harker, and the fact that that very morning, King had been found dead in the swimming pool exactly as depicted in the dream.

In the end the doctor shook his head. 'He certainly didn't mention anything about that when I saw him on Monday.'

'Did he seem to be worried about anything . . . were there any signs of depression?'

'No, Inspector. Not at all. On the contrary, he was very businesslike and forward-looking. I remember him saying, quite light-heartedly at his desk, that he would go to the office that day even if he had to crawl there on his hands and knees.'

Angel rubbed his chin. It was difficult to reconcile the fact that the witnesses expressed widely different opinions as to Haydn King's state of mind.

'Do you think King had been acting a part,' Angel said, 'making a show of being trouble-free when all the time the dream was grinding away at him?'

'It's possible. The dream may have been worrying him — even frightening him — we will never know.'

Angel nodded. 'If some of us didn't have secrets, we'd go mad,' he said.

'The brain is a highly complicated organ,' Doctor Singh said. 'Also there are far too many things of this world and the next of which we know nothing. You know, Inspector, I have often thought that in cases that end in tragedy, like this, the subject could have been suicidal and willing death upon themselves. However, in this instance, I cannot see it happening with a subject like Mr King. He was far too strong-willed and involved with his work.'

Angel rubbed his chin. 'What part do you think the recurring dream played in the finding of his body in the swimming pool? It can't be marked down as unconnected.'

'I don't know, Inspector. I really don't know.'

'How would you have treated Mr King if he had been to see you complaining of such a dream?'

Dr Singh pursed his lips. 'It would have depended upon the way he presented himself at the time of the consultation,' he said. 'I would probably have prescribed a tranquilizer to begin with, and suggested that he took a holiday, well away from the swimming pool.'

Angel stood up. 'Thank you, Doctor. Thank you very much.'

At the door, Angel turned back and said, 'Hey, Doctor. One last question. Would you have directed him to consult a psychiatrist?'

Dr Singh swivelled the chair round to face him and, with a furrowed brow, said, 'I wouldn't have been in any hurry, Inspector, although it is difficult to answer the question hypothetically. I have in my armoury a range of medicines as well as non-medical therapies which might have been appropriate to explore.'

Angel considered the reply for a few moments then nodded in agreement.

Then Singh said, 'Anyway, I doubt very much if Mr King would have agreed to see a psychiatrist.'

Angel gave the doctor a wry smile and shook his head. He closed the surgery door and went down the corridor packed with patients waiting for evening surgery to begin.

He went out into the cold, dark night to the BMW parked in the surgery car park. He slumped into the driving seat and looked through the frost-covered windscreen into the night. He was thinking. He was convinced in his own mind that Haydn King had been murdered and, although the house had been securely locked and there were no signs of a break-in, there were a lot of keys in circulation. Besides Mr King, there was Meredith the butler, Mrs Selina Johnson the housekeeper, Harry Saw the private secretary and Vincent Fleming the nephew, who all had keys. Also the back-door key was left in the lock. By arrangement, an accomplice could easily have left the door unlocked. It would only have taken a few moments for an intruder to enter the kitchen area and relock the door.

SEVEN

Angel arrived home at seven o'clock. He was an hour and a half late.

'Hello, love,' he said.

Mary wasn't pleased. She glared at him as if he was the gasman who had come to cut off the supply.

He went into the hall, took off his coat, hung it in the lobby and returned to the kitchen.

'Well, I don't know what your tea will be like,' she said. 'All shrivelled up, I expect.'

He didn't reply. He could see how things were. Whatever he said would be wrong. He reached into the fridge for a bottle of beer.

After a measured amount of silence, she said, 'Why didn't you phone?'

He wrinkled his nose. 'You know what it's like,' he said.

'No, I don't know what it's like. How long does it take to phone? And fish doesn't come cheap anymore. Those two pieces cost over five pounds.'

He blinked. 'Five pounds? It's time you changed your fishmonger.'

'I have. Twice. There's nobody cheaper than "Cheapo's". Finny haddock is expensive *everywhere*.'

Angel pulled open a drawer and took out a bottle opener. He prised off the metal cap, poured the beer into a glass then sat down at the table.

Mary approached the oven with an oven glove. She took out the plates and then served up the fish.

Angel looked at the steaming, golden-coloured finny haddock in melted butter. It looked delicious and was far from being dried up.

With several slices of wholemeal bread, he soon cleared his plate, while Mary was still eating.

'That was great,' he said as he put the knife and fork together. 'Thank you, love.'

Under those particular circumstances, he wouldn't have said anything different. However, on this occasion as on virtually every occasion, it was true. Mary's cooking was unbeatable. And somehow she had rescued the meal from a shrivelled-up disaster.

Although angry, she was pleased he had enjoyed it. And she could always tell if he wasn't telling the truth.

She nodded, swallowed and said, 'There's fresh fruit salad and ice cream to follow.' She knew that that would please him. He loved ice cream.

'Right,' he said, sitting back in the chair, content to wait until she had caught up with him.

Mary Angel would never have told him, but she had always secretly compared him to the late, great Johnny Weissmuller. Angel was in great shape, but Mary, who was always seeking for perfection, thought that the loss of a few pounds might improve him.

As she took another mouthful, she gave him a sideways glance. Then something occurred to her. The corners of her mouth turned momentarily into a smile. It promptly disappeared; her eyes twinkled mischievously as she said, 'Or you could skip the ice cream.'

He looked across at her. He knew she was teasing him. 'No,' he said, keeping a straight face. 'That's all right, Mary. I'll force it down, if necessary.'

Their eyes met, and they both grinned.

After the fruit and ice cream, they moved out of the kitchen to the sitting room where Mary brought in the coffee.

Angel switched on the TV for the latest news and caught the end of an item about the London stock market closing down forty points due to a drop of the Dow Jones in the US, and some banks and King's Breweries in the UK.

His eyes opened wide and he stared at the TV screen.

The newsreader said, 'The dip in the closing price of King's Breweries was brought about by the sudden death of King's Breweries Chairman, Haydn King, who was found dead of a heart attack in his swimming pool at his home in Bromersley, South Yorkshire, early this morning. And that is the end of the business news. Now over to Carol for the weather.'

Angel's face creased, then his eyes opened wide in wonderment. 'I wonder how that leaked out?' he muttered. He reached out for the TV remote and pressed the 'off' button.

Mary looked up from the coffee. 'So that's the case you are working on?'

Angel looked at her curiously. 'How did you know?' he said.

She smiled. 'It's all over the news, the dead man is local, and you come home late. Therefore I guessed that Harker had pushed the case onto you because the poor man probably didn't die naturally and there's something fishy about it.'

'You never cease to amaze me,' he said, taking a sip of the coffee.

'You're my husband, Michael, and I can also see beneath all this superficiality that your brain is fully engaged. I've seen you like this hundreds of times.'

He waved a hand in the air. 'But no announcement about his death has been made. I've not been approached by anybody from the media.'

'Is it a big secret, then?'

'Not particularly. It's just that . . . nobody can possibly know what Haydn King died from. I'm in charge of the investigation, and even I don't know. The post-mortem has not yet been completed. And fishy? You said fishy. What's fishy about it?'

She shrugged. 'I don't know,' she said. 'It doesn't seem right, being found in a swimming pool early in the morning in the middle of winter, I suppose.'

Angel shook his head, then he said, 'Mary, my love, you haven't heard the half of it.'

He repeated the story Superintendent Harker had told him about being summoned by Haydn King and the conversation that had taken place on Tuesday evening between the two of them; three days before King was found dead in the pool.

'If it had been anybody other than the super,' Angel said, 'I might not have believed it.'

She listened carefully to him and when he had finished, she said, 'Michael, it seems to me that something was preying on his mind, and that maybe he wanted to take his own life.'

He rubbed his chin. 'It doesn't seem to be his style. I've asked around.'

'But the nightmares were worrying him. That's why he called Superintendent Harker in.'

'That's part of the puzzle. Only his butler and the super know anything about them.'

Mary shook her head and frowned.

'He hadn't told his doctor,' Angel said. 'And he saw him on Monday about something else — a touch of gout — but he never mentioned nightmares.'

Mary shook her head. 'That rules out the likelihood then, that some enemy of Haydn King made the dreams a reality by murdering him in the belief that it would be assumed that his death was suicide?'

'I agree. Most definitely, it does,' he said, then he frowned, looked at her and added, 'What a convoluted train of thought.'

'I get it from living with you,' she said.

He smiled.

She frowned then, pensively, she said, 'There's something else, Michael.'

He looked at her closely. Sometimes his wife came out with astonishingly original suggestions.

She hesitated.

'What, love?' he said. 'Come on, spit it out.'

'Isn't it possible that whoever wanted to see Haydn King dead, was a hypnotist — not necessarily a super-duper properly qualified hypnotist, but someone who knows how hypnotism works? . . . somebody who had the gift of being able to plant an idea in Mr King's mind . . . then when he'd tormented him enough, went on to convince him that the only way to stop the dream was to fulfil it by . . . by jumping off the diving board . . . landing deliberately badly and whoosh, seconds later he'd be dead, out of this world.'

Angel stared at her. He rubbed his chin. He breathed heavily a couple of times then said, 'It's a bit extreme, that, Mary.'

'But do you think it's possible?'

He gave a little shrug. 'It's possible, I suppose, yes. But King was a man with a powerful personality. Not easily swayed, you know.'

She nodded. 'You could get some expert advice.'

'Mmmm. I'll have to think about that, love. You might have a point, though.'

She noticed his cup was empty. 'More coffee?'

He passed the cup. 'Please.' Then he added, 'I will have to go in tomorrow. I can't leave this while Monday. For one thing, I want to look over King's house. There might be something that will give me a lead.'

Meredith pushed the open door and said, 'And this was Mr King's bedroom, sir. I still find it difficult to accept that he has gone. I instructed the housekeeper to give the room an especially good clean round after your men had finished yesterday afternoon.'

Angel looked round. Everything certainly looked tidy, shiny and spotlessly clean. Suddenly he caught sight of a paperback book on the bedside table. He crossed quickly and leaned over to read the title. It was *The Interpretation of Dreams* by Sigmund Freud.

Angel pursed his lips. He immediately thought about the conversation he'd had with Mary last evening and the suggestion she had made. Didn't Freud make scientific investigations into hypnosis? This paperback could be very important.

Angel turned to Meredith and said, 'Where did that book come from?'

Meredith reached out to pick it up.

'Please don't touch it,' Angel said.

Meredith withdrew his hand, gave him a strange look, then peered down at the book, read the title and said, 'Do you know, sir, I really have no idea.'

Angel took a rolled-up A4-sized polythene envelope with the word EVIDENCE printed across it in big red letters out of his pocket. With a pencil, he skilfully edged the book into the bag, then he sealed it and slid it into his pocket. He then turned back to Meredith and said, 'How long has it been there?'

'I am not sure. I had no reason to take much notice.'

'No,' Angel said, rubbing his chin. He had another quick look round. 'Are there any other books in the room?'

Meredith turned his head to the left and then the right, then said, 'No, I don't believe there are.'

Angel looked under the bed, pulled out all the drawers of a large tallboy, peered through the window that opened onto a balcony and had an extensive view of lawns and trees, and opened the door of a walk-in wardrobe the width of the room. It was dark inside. He found the light switch, went inside, prodded a few suits, came out and said, 'Thank you. I think I've seen all I want to see here.'

Meredith then moved on to show Angel the next bedroom.

Angel came out of Haydn King's bedroom, turned right to the next room and tried the doorknob. The door was locked.

Meredith came forward while his hand followed down a gilt-coloured chain from a button on his trouser waistband to his pocket. At the end of the chain was a bunch of keys. 'This is the late Mrs Lydia King's bedroom, sir. Mr Haydn's mother. Mr King kept it locked because he said he wanted to keep it private. He had the only other key, of course. He didn't want anybody but me to go into it and then only for essential reasons. I vacuum and dust it every week.'

Meredith unlocked the door and pushed it open. Angel walked in and looked round.

It was a bright, double-windowed room, immaculately decorated and carpeted, furnished with a large half tester bed draped with intricately embroidered curtains, a built-in wardrobe and a huge dressing-table covered with many containers of powder, foundation and perfumes. The décor was in matching pastel colours. In a corner was a wheelchair, a Zimmer frame and a pair of aluminium elbow crutches. There was a door out of the bedroom leading to an en-suite, fully tiled bathroom fitted with all the usual modern facilities. King's mother seemed to have lacked nothing in her latter days.

'Mr King used to come in here for hours at a time, sir,' Meredith said. 'I don't know quite what he did, but I think it gave him solace.'

Angel turned to Meredith and said, 'Really?' He rubbed his chin.

Meredith nodded.

After a last look round, Angel said, 'Thank you. I've seen enough. Can we move on?'

They came out of the room. Meredith carefully locked the door and returned the key on the chain to his trouser pocket. He showed Angel the other rather spartan bedrooms and bathrooms on the first floor, then brought him down in the lift to the ground floor to see King's study, the other reception rooms, and a large dining-room. Then down in the lift to the basement to the kitchen, pantry, butler's pantry, cold room, fuel store and staff dining-room.

Angel found the house an appropriately appointed luxury family house, but apart from some items in King's bedroom found nothing useful in solving the mystery of the man's death. At length he thanked the butler and returned to the BMW.

He started the car and drove down the long drive to the gate and out into Pine Avenue and onto Creesforth Road.

It was a gloomy moody sky and the cold squally wind wouldn't let him forget that it was already December. In ten days it would be shortest day and in thirteen it would be Christmas. If he went home that afternoon, Mary would almost certainly drag him out to the shops and that was something he would rather avoid.

He was thinking about this as he drove past the park gates, when he suddenly had the urge to see his friend Dr Mac, the pathologist. That might, he thought, clarify his thinking and perhaps help him make better sense of the puzzle.

Mac worked in the mortuary in Bromersley General Hospital, but being Saturday, Angel reasoned, he might not have chosen to turn out.

Angel turned left off Park Road, took two more left turns through an estate of terrace houses, then a right which took him the opposite way along Park Road and direct to the hospital gates. Parking was always difficult at Bromersley General Hospital and, as Saturday was a big visiting day, finding a space was difficult. However, he was fortunate and was able to drive into a space as someone was leaving.

He locked the car, entered the hospital by the revolving door and made his way on the ground floor to the far end of a long corridor to the MORTUARY. The door was locked, which was no surprise to him. It was always so. Access was gained by ringing a bell. In the past, dead bodies had been known to go missing.

He pressed the bell push. As soon as his finger came off the button, he felt convinced that he wouldn't get any response. He felt certain that dear old Mac was at that very moment being dragged round Tesco's or Marks & Spencer or some other emporium by his ever-loving spouse.

He wrinkled his nose, turned away and began the trudge away down the corridor, when he heard the sound of a door opening behind him. He turned round.

A small man in a green overall, wellington boots and a tight white hat was standing in the open door of the mortuary. 'Hey, Michael!' he called. 'Is it you playing push and run with this bell?'

It was Mac.

Angel's face brightened. 'Guilty,' he said. He turned and walked back up to him. 'What are you doing here on a Saturday afternoon?' he said. 'Got a woman in there?'

Mac grinned. 'I've got two,' he said, patting Angel lightly on the back. 'Come on in and take one off my hands.'

'I thought you'd be out shopping with your missus for that special little Christmas gift for your Aunt Ada,' Angel said.

He followed Mac inside and closed the door.

'I haven't got an Aunt Ada,' Mac said.

Angel smiled. 'Well, Gladys then. Or Hermione.'

Mac nodded knowingly and led Angel into his small office and pointed to a chair. Angel sat down.

'My wife knows better than to try and get me on that kick, Michael,' Mac said, sitting down in the swivel chair behind his desk. 'I give her the money and she trots off and does it.'

Angel raised his eyebrows. 'I wish Mary would do that.'

'Takes years of married life,' Mac said.

Angel grinned. 'I'm sure, but I haven't come here for a lecture on how to manage a wife.'

'You've come here to get out of shopping with her.'

'Certainly not. She's at home, busy baking something. *You* know why I'm here.'

Mac nodded. 'You want to know what he died from. And the time. Well, it's taken me a bit longer to calculate time of death because I had to take readings not only of the temperature in different parts of the pool, but also the volume of the water and the circulation pattern of it. And I can now say with reasonable certainty that he died between 11 p.m. Thursday night and 4 a.m., yesterday morning. And the cause "looks like" a severe blow to the head causing an internal haemorrhage. I stress the words "looks like".'

'Not drowning?'

'Might have been a contributory factor.'

'Any idea what the instrument administering the blow might have been?'

'Something heavy with a hard edge to it.'

'Is it consistent with him diving into the pool, crashing into the edge of the pool and then falling into the water?'

'Aye, but I can't say for certain that that's what happened. There might be other factors. I may know more after I have examined the major organs.'

The muscles round Angel's mouth tightened. 'How on earth could Haydn King have dreamt two days before he died, that *that's* how it would happen?'

Mac frowned and turned back to him. 'What do you mean?'

Angel told him about the nightmare.

When he had finished, Mac said, 'It's nae possible!'

Angel shrugged. 'They are the facts, Mac. If it's not possible, you're suggesting that the dead man or the super were lying. What motive could either of them have had?'

Mac rubbed his chin.

'It's got me beat,' Angel said.

Mac said, 'King could have been hypnotized.'

'Mary said that last night,' Angel said. 'Do you think that a seriously busy man like Haydn King would get himself involved with a hypnotist?'

'Canna think of any other explanation.'

Anyway, I have always been given to understand that a person hypnotized would not do anything that was out of character.'

Mac nodded. 'Aye. I'm sure that's right, Michael.'

'Well, I have no evidence to suggest that Haydn King wanted to kill himself.'

Mac sighed. After a few moments, he said, 'I'm glad I'm working with scientific facts . . . with things I can see and touch. I'd be no good doing your job, trying to discover a baddie among all the goodies.'

'I also rely on forensic to some extent,' Angel said with a twinkle in his eye. '*You* know that.'

'I'm glad I have my uses. Do you want to know what I've got so far?'

'That's what I've come for,' he said, rising from the chair.

Mac nodded. 'I've hardly started. Come on through. I'm recording it.'

They reached the examination theatre. The walls and floor were covered with white tiles. In addition, the floor had a gradient toward the far side to an open drain with a grate to the sewer in the corner. In the centre of the floor, on a rubber-topped examination table was the naked body of Haydn King. He was stretched out and partly covered by a sheet. A powerful battery of white strip lights was suspended over the table. Hanging just below them was a microphone that led to a small cassette recorder on an instrument table at the side.

As Angel entered, his nose went upwards and his face creased at the indescribable smell of ammonia combined with odours only dead humans could generate.

Mac pulled on a pair of surgical gloves and lifted his mask up to cover his nose and mouth. He leaned over to the side table, pressed a couple of switches, then said, 'There. I'll play back what I recorded nobbut five minutes ago.'

His voice, sounding more Scots than he did in real life, came through the recorder: 'Body of a man taken from swimming pool at approximately 0800 hours, Friday, December 9, 2011. Understood to be Haydn King. Weight 182 pounds. Height 6 feet. Aged about fifty. Brown eyes. Black beard and a full head of hair. Good physique. Has a suntan . . . wearing off. Must have spent time in a warmer clime recently. No distinguishing marks, tattoos, jewellery, body-piercing or the like. Hands regularly manicured. External examination. Severe abrasion to head resulting in compacted cranium and heavily fractured skull. Old appendix scar. No other external wound or abrasion visible to the naked eye.'

Mac leaned across and turned the recorder off. 'That's as far as I got.'

Angel shook his head. 'Nothing there to make a case out of,' he said with a sniff. 'Any signs of the use of a needle?'

Mac looked at him over his spectacles. 'Do ye mean was he a druggie?'

Angel gave the slightest hint of a shrug. 'No. I didn't exactly mean, did he inject himself with a conventional street drug, Mac. I know that'll be in your PM in due course. I meant, was there any sign that he had had a . . . well, a jab of a different sort, the last hour or so of his life?'

Mac slowly shook his head and smiled. 'Now what's going through that complex, devious mind of yours?'

'Well, Mac, there are a fair few million pounds looking for a new home right now. And I just wondered if King's thinking processes had been . . . er, interfered with.'

'You mean, by the injection of a hypnotic drug by a wayward psychologist, hypnotist, trick cyclist or some such character?'

'That's what I was thinking . . . who might then have talked King into killing himself?'

'Something like that. I know it sounds unlikely, a man with the strong character he is reputed to have had, but there might just be a bruise, wound or reaction mark where the finest needle might have been furtively introduced.'

'I haven't checked that, Michael, yet, but I certainly will.'

'Thanks, Mac.'

EIGHT

Angel had a peaceful Saturday evening and Sunday at home.

It became apparent that Mary had already taken care of the Christmas present shopping during the week, and was at that time busy wrapping them, for which he was truly thankful. It allowed him time to sit in front of the fire with the television on, reading through and putting into good English his findings in connection with the Haydn King case, and the report of the distinctive dead blonde woman seen in the area behind the King George Hotel.

Every so often, Mary came into the sitting room to show him what gift she had chosen for a particular member of the family. She said that that was so that he could look intelligent if any of them were to thank him. He knew that it was actually to enrol his support for whatever she had bought, and many a time he thought the gift absolutely wacky. But whatever it was, he always tried to look interested and make encouraging noises.

And so the weekend soon passed.

It was 8.28 a.m., Monday, 12 December.

Angel was making his way down the station corridor to his office.

He had only just removed his coat, scarf and hat and was pulling the swivel chair up to his desk when there was a knock at the door. It was Ahmed. He was carrying a yellow file.

'What is it, lad?'

'Copy of a deposition from the super, sir,' he said, handing him the file.

Angel blinked. He was thinking that Harker had dealt with it unusually promptly. It had only been mentioned on Friday afternoon. He glanced inside. There were two A4 sheets of double-spaced typing. He closed the file, put it down on the desk and looked up at the young man. 'Ah yes,' he said. 'Thank you.'

Ahmed said, 'And I have done a search on the PNC, sir, and there is nothing known about Haydn King.'

'Right, Ahmed,' he said. Then he frowned and looked up. 'Didn't I ask DS Crisp to make *that* search?'

'He asked me to do it on Friday, sir. He had to go out to Harbottle & Haig, the stockbrokers.'

Angel wasn't pleased. He shook his head and blew out a yard of breath. He was thinking that Crisp had no right to delegate. But he fully realized the merit of selective delegation to someone reliable. He gave a little shrug. He wished he could delegate more, but he knew he couldn't.

'Right lad,' he said with a nod.

Ahmed turned towards the door.

'Just a minute, lad. Phone Wakefield, NCOF and see if they have access to a specialist on hypnotism.'

Ahmed looked puzzled. 'Hypnotism, sir?'

'I know it's unlikely but I've got to start there.'

'What's the NCOF, sir?'

Angel shook his head impatiently. 'You'll have to learn these acronyms off by heart, lad, you've been a fully-fledged copper now nigh-on four years. You need to look intelligent when you're up with the oldies. It's the National Crime Operations Faculty. Remember that. The police unit of men and women who are experts in their field.'

'Right, sir.'

'And have you finished checking out King's mobile phone and his house phone?'

'Not yet, sir.'

'I know you're always very careful, Ahmed, but I want you to be particularly meticulous. Don't let a single call be bypassed if it is in any way unusual. And I'd like your results as soon as ever possible.'

'Right, sir,' Ahmed said, and he went out.

Angel turned to thinking he could do with Crisp's report on the financial state of King's Breweries and Haydn King in particular. He was of a mind to put a rocket up that lad's backside. He reached out for the phone, when there was a knock at the door.

'Come in,' he called.

It was DS Carter. She came in smiling. She was usually smiling and always agreeable.

'Good morning, sir. I've got that info you wanted,' she said, pulling her notebook out of the bag slung over her shoulder.

Angel managed a fleeting, reciprocal smile. He replaced the phone. He pointed at the chair opposite him. She sat down.

He recalled that he had asked her to find out the contents of King's last will and testament and he was keen to hear what she had found out.

'Right, lass. What you got?'

'King's solicitor is Mr Bloomfield,' she said, opening the notebook.

He knew him well. Angel thought him to be probably the most conscientious solicitor in the town.

'He let me read Mr King's last will. It was dated July 11th this year. Apart from relatively small bequests, including ten thousand pounds to Nicholas Fitzroy Meredith, his butler for more than twenty years, the bulk of the shares in King's Breweries, the house on Pine Avenue, the house in Florida, the boat and other stocks and shares will go to his nephew, Vincent Fleming.'

'Wow!' Angel said. He pursed his lips. 'That makes Fleming a multi-millionaire.'

'*Yes*, sir,' she said.

Angel rubbed his chin slowly. He had a lot to think about. 'Right, Flora. Thank you.'

'But there's more, sir,' she said. She opened her eyes wider to emphasize the point.

He raised an open hand, making a gesture inviting her to continue.

She turned a page in her notebook and said, 'There was a new will prepared by Mr Bloomfield at Mr King's request. It was to change that one substantially. The small bequests remained the same, except for that to Nicholas Fitzroy Meredith, who was to receive the bulk of the estate. Vincent Fleming was to receive nothing.'

Angel raised his eyebrows. 'But it was not signed?'

'No, sir. Mr Bloomfield said that Mr King had given him instructions over the phone about ten days ago, and he had an appointment to sign it on the Monday, but phoned in to cancel because he was ill.'

Angel had a thought. He hurriedly pulled some envelopes out of his inside pocket and glanced through them. He found what he wanted. He looked up at Flora and said, 'It adds up. That was the day he had gout.'

She nodded. 'Mr Bloomfield said that he offered to come up to Mr King's office or his house with a clerk as a witness, but Mr King declined. He said that he would phone Mr Bloomfield back in a few days to make another appointment. Of course, he never did. There's going to be one very lucky man following Haydn King's coffin to the Mount Pleasant Crematorium in the near future.'

Angel shook his head slowly, pursed his lips again and said, 'Aye. And one very unlucky one.' Then he added, 'Did Bloomfield tell you why Fleming suddenly fell out of King's favour?'

'No, sir. King didn't offer any explanation and Bloomfield knew better — I suppose — than to ask him.'

Angel's eyes narrowed. It would be interesting to know what made King change his mind.

The phone rang. Angel reached out for it. It was Superintendent Harker. There was the usual coughing and then he said, 'I want you to make yourself available this afternoon, Angel. There's a DI Mathew Elliott from the Antiques and Fine Art squad, London, coming up. He was coming to see me at two o'clock. It's about a link between a murder case he's involved with in Hackney and a possible suspect from around here. All sounds very vague and probably a waste of time. Didn't have any names in mind to offer so you can't look anything up before he gets here. Now, as it happens, I have an appointment at the hospital at two o'clock, an operation that'll keep me away all afternoon. They're shoving a camera into me in a very particular place, and I'm not looking forward to it. So I'll have to leave this chap with you. Give him my apologies and look after him. Make him feel welcome. You never know when we might need to reciprocate.'

'Right, sir,' Angel said. 'We've been in touch with Mathew Elliott before, sir. But in those days he was a sergeant . . .'

There was an abrupt click and the line went dead. Harker had replaced the phone.

Angel's eyebrows shot up. He gritted his teeth and looked at the receiver.

Flora saw his face and said, 'Everything all right, sir?'

Anybody would think Harker was running Marks & Spencer, Angel thought.

'The super was in rather a hurry, that's all,' he said.

He returned the receiver to its cradle. Two seconds later, the phone rang again.

He looked at it, wrinkled his nose and picked it up. 'Angel.'

A small male voice said, 'This is PC Knightly on reception, sir. Sorry to bother you. There's a woman here from that posh dress shop down the arcade, Madam Vera's . . . the one that was broken into last week. She wants to see whoever's in charge of the investigation. I take it that that's you, sir?'

Angel sighed. 'Yes, lad, it is, but I'm extremely busy just now. What does she want?'

'I don't know exactly, sir. I think she er . . .' At this point the young policeman lowered his voice to a whisper. 'I think she just wants to chivvy you up, sir. She says the break-in has cost her a lot of money, and she's hoping for "restoration", as she put it.'

'And I'm hoping to win the lottery,' Angel said.

'What's that, sir?'

'Never mind, lad. I'll sort it. Ask her to wait there a few minutes.'

He replaced the phone and turned to Flora.

'Madam Vera, or whatever her real name is, is in reception. Find out from Don Taylor if he found any forensic at her shop, also check on whether there was anything useful from any CCTV in the area. Then nip up to reception and see what she has to say . . . and find out what exactly was stolen. A PC has already taken the details, but take them again. You're a woman; you'll have a better idea about the value and significance of the theft. Indeed, if there is any. Maybe get a lead on what sort of a person would rob an expensive dress shop. Say, an angry disappointed customer . . . or someone with a grudge, you know. Personally I don't know why women get so animated about such relatively trivial things as what they wear.'

It was Flora's turn to raise her eyebrows. 'Well *you* obviously care, sir. I mean, you always look very smart.'

'Well, it's the expected uniform for a police inspector's job, isn't it? How can anyone go wrong with a clean, pressed dark suit, cotton shirt, tie and polished black leather shoes.'

'Don't you ever want a change?'

'Huh. You'd think I was a right berk if I turned up here in a bright green jacket, tartan trousers and a red shirt, wouldn't you? Now hop off find out what you can and settle Madam Vera down. I feel a bit guilty about neglecting her . . . but there just isn't enough time.'

Flora went out and closed the door.

Angel looked up at the clock. It said 10.20 a.m. He fumbled in the bottom of his jacket pocket and came out with two business cards. He put one back in his pocket and put the other one on his desk in front of him. He reached out for the phone, looked down and tapped in the number he read off the card. The phone was soon answered by a voice that sounded like a desperate young mermaid whose vocal cords had been marinated in honey.

'Vincent Fleming Associates, insurance brokers,' she said. 'Can I help you?'

His eyebrows went up. 'This is Detective Inspector Angel,' he said. 'I want to speak to Mr Fleming, please.'

'Oh yes. Thank you, Inspector. Won't keep you a moment.'

Fleming came on the line. He seemed very buoyant. 'Why, good morning, Inspector. What a pleasant surprise. And what can I do for you?'

'I need to see you straightaway, Mr Fleming.'

'Dear me. It sounds serious. Well, I am at your disposal, Inspector.'

Eight minutes later Angel was sitting in Fleming's ground-floor office in an office block in the centre of Bromersley on the corner of Huddersfield Road and Karl Marx Row.

'Have you come to tell me that you have completed your inquiries into my uncle's death, Inspector?' Fleming said.

Angel rubbed his chin. 'Not quite,' he said. 'But I am getting there. Have you been in touch with Mr Bloomfield, your uncle's solicitor?'

'Ah, I see where you are going with this, Inspector. No, but Bloomfield rang me on Friday afternoon to offer his condolences and to tell me that I had inherited the bulk of my Uncle Haydn's estate. However I would rather have had my uncle alive . . . to enjoy his friendship and guidance . . . after all, he was my nearest relative. But naturally the fact that he left me so provided for . . . was solace to me at this dreadful time.'

'You speak of your uncle with affection, but did you get on well with him?'

'You will understand, my dear Inspector, that Uncle Haydn was, in modern parlance, a self-made man. He was king in attitude as well as in name. He started with very little and because most of his commercial decisions were spot on, his business was successful and grew to the size it is. Thereafter, he tended to assume an air of infallibility. So it was understandable that he might disagree with people who had divergent opinions.'

Angel pursed his lips. 'Are you saying you *didn't* get on with him?'

'On the contrary, Inspector. We got on very well most of the time, but there were times when he could be . . . erm, difficult.'

'Did he complain to you about the strange dreams — or nightmares, you could call them — he had been having over the past two weeks?'

'Nightmares?' he said with a grin. 'No. Certainly not. This is the first I've heard of that. Tell me about them.'

'Did you find him behaving differently over the past two weeks? Was he morose, introspective or depressed?'

'Not at all. I would have noticed. He invited me for dinner that last Thursday evening, and I was with him for about three hours. I'm pretty certain that if there had been anything like that worrying him, he would have told me about it then.'

'What time did you leave?'

'Must have been about 9.30. Uncle Haydn didn't keep late hours.'

'What did you talk about?'

'The same as always. Business. I am an insurance broker. He had been considering putting his insurance, both business and personal, through me. We talked about the sort of cover he would need and the cost.'

'Would that have amounted to much?'

'The commission would have been eleven or twelve thousand pounds a year. Very welcome in these difficult times, Inspector.'

Angel nodded. He pursed his lips. Eleven thousand pounds was a large amount of money, but not life-changing, he thought.

'He had carefully arranged them so that they were all due for renewal on the first day of the year,' Fleming said. He wanted to be sure that he was getting the very best deal before he put the suggestion to his co-directors. Of course they would pretty well rubber-stamp anything my uncle said, but he didn't want any of them finding a better deal somewhere else and then be accused of nepotism.'

'Of course. Anything else?'

'Well, we talked about the weather, the brewing business . . . Auntie Judy, I should say ex-Auntie Judy.'

'Judy Savage? What about her?'

'She was annoying him. She had apparently instructed her solicitor to write to him to say that she couldn't manage on the allowance the judge had agreed he should pay and that she was appealing through the court for a substantial increase.'

'How much was that disturbing him?'

'It was annoying him. It was making him angry with her, very angry indeed. But she was wasting her time.'

'It wouldn't keep him awake at nights?'

'Oh no. I wouldn't have thought so. Not at all.'

'And what did he say about the brewing business?'

'He was saying how well everything was going. He was bursting with optimism. He said that he expected to deliver the best balance sheet the brewery had ever known.'

Angel rubbed his chin. Those were definitely not the thoughts and attitudes of a man considering taking his own life. He shook his head and screwed up his eyes. He was no further forward in solving the mystery of the dreams.

However, he thought that this was time for him to drop the bombshell on Vincent Fleming and watch his reaction.

'Did you know,' Angel said, 'that about ten days ago your uncle gave instructions to Mr Bloomfield to take you out of the will and put Mr Meredith there in your stead? And that Bloomfield had prepared a new will ready for your uncle's signature, but he never signed it?'

Fleming blinked. His jaw dropped. He stared at Angel. It looked as if he hadn't known.

Angel said, 'What exactly happened ten days ago?'

Fleming licked his lips. His eyes narrowed and he looked in the direction of the skirting board at the opposite side of the office, while slowly shaking his head.

Angel waited.

Eventually Fleming breathed out a heavy sigh, looked at Angel and said, 'You've really bowled me a googly there, Angel, old chap.'

Angel held out his hands palms upward to indicate that it had not been his intention.

Fleming shrugged. 'So I was to be left out, was I?' The muscles round his mouth tightened. 'That would be *dear* Aunt Judy,' he said.

His face showed that he held her very far from 'dear'.

'Uncle Haydn phoned me ten days ago breathing brimstone and fire about her. He thought that I had some allegiance towards her. About the time of the divorce and several times afterwards, she visited me, and she used to ring me up seeking consolation. He might have thought that I was being disloyal . . . even a spy in the camp. There wasn't an atom of truth in it, but I could hardly tell her to go away. It's odd that he didn't mention the will at all on Thursday evening.'

'Did *you* tell him that you had been in touch with her?'

'Oh no. I expect he would have found out either directly from her, or she may have confided in her own solicitor and that had been conveyed to Bloomfield, who had dutifully informed my uncle. I don't know.' He shook his head. 'But I am surprised, Inspector, that something so relatively trivial would have such extreme consequences.'

Angel wrinkled his nose. At that time, nothing surprised him.

NINE

The interview with Vincent Fleming had in no way progressed Angel's investigation into Haydn King's death, nor had it assisted him in understanding the influence of the nightmares conveyed to him by Superintendent Harker and confirmed by King's butler, Meredith. To say that Angel was disappointed would be to putting it mildly.

He came out of Fleming's office and drove the BMW to the car park of the Fat Duck, and, as he kicked his way through an inch of snow to the pub door, he thought about Vincent Fleming. Coming into that mammoth inheritance could make Fleming look as guilty as hell, if he had known that his uncle had intended changing his will.

The pub wasn't busy. At the bar he ordered a roast beef sandwich and a pint of shandy, which he enjoyed in silence while thinking about the case.

Fleming had a front door key to King's house. He could easily have entered in the middle of the night. He could have crept into the swimming pool room, waited behind the cubicle curtain and with whatever weapon it was, murdered King before he had time to get down to Bloomfield's to append his signature to the new will.

He mulled over the matter for a while. There was motive *and* opportunity, but at that moment no weapon, and not an atom of proof.

He returned to his office at 1.50. He hung up his coat and reached out for the phone. He tapped in the extension number for SOCO. It was answered by DS Taylor.

'Don,' Angel said. 'You have a book, taken from Haydn King's bedroom: *The Interpretation of Dreams*. You were checking it for fingerprints.'

'Yes, sir,' Taylor said. 'I haven't had the chance to get to it yet . . . there's so much.'

'I know. I know. I want you to deal with it by the end of the day. Verbal would be OK. The written can follow.'

'Right, sir. What exactly do you need?'

'I need to know specifically whose prints are on it, that's all. I'll phone you first thing in the morning.'

'Righto, sir,' Taylor said.

Before Angel could return the phone to its cradle, there was a knock at the door.

'Come in,' he called. It was DI Mathew Elliott of the Art and Antiques squad, a smart, handsome young man in a dark suit, white shirt and tie.

Angel smiled broadly. 'Ah, Mathew,' he said. 'I believe congratulations are in order. It's a couple of years since we last met. You were a sergeant then. I hear that you've now reached the dizzy heights of inspector.'

Elliott grinned. 'A few more quid in the pay packet, you know, sir. Still not in your class, though.'

'Nay, Mathew. And call me Michael for goodness sake. And there's no need to ingratiate yourself now that we're the same rank.'

Elliott laughed. 'You don't change, at all.'

Angel pointed to the chair and said, 'Sit down, lad, and tell me what brings you out of your plush London HQ where it's all happening, to this backwater?'

When he was settled, Elliott said, 'Well, Michael, you will have heard about the robbery of that diamond-and-ruby Rosary?'

Angel nodded. The newspapers had been full of it.

'Well,' Elliott said, 'we have reason to believe that it might be somewhere round here. And I want to enrol your help to find it.'

Angel's eyebrows went up. 'Well, Mathew, I'll do what I can.'

'We know the Rosary was stolen by a gang of three. The gang leader was a big man by the name of James Argyle, aged fifty. A Scot. Specs. Tubby. He had a short black beard turning ginger. A woman, playing the part of his wife, was Marcia Moore, aged thirty-five, but looking younger. A real eye-knocker. More curves than Silverstone. Big blonde hair. Permanent pout. Eyes always half-shut. Well-known prostitute and good-time girl. For the third one, the driver, the description is vague, as he was not seen much by any witnesses. However, we think it may be Freddie Jay, aged fifty. Are any of those known to you?'

'If it is the same woman, she was seen in a scruffy hotel in town. The King George Hotel. It should never be called a hotel. I wouldn't board my cat there. It might catch something and it wouldn't be a mouse.'

'When was this, Michael?'

'It would be the evening of the day of the robbery, Wednesday.'

'Ah yes. You wouldn't have a photograph of her?'

He shook his head. 'It's not the sort of hotel that has CCTV.'

'But it sounds like the sort of place where she would work.'

'She was reported dead, but also seen after that, very much alive and kicking.'

Elliott frowned. 'Strange,' he said.

Angel nodded. 'I'm still working on it,' he said. 'Anyway, what have you got that links them to this patch?'

'I'll tell you. That Wednesday night, about ten hours after the robbery, an elderly newspaper-seller who worked near Hatton Garden called Dermot O'Leary had his neck broken and was then unceremoniously dumped in the empty bath in his bathroom. His flat was thoroughly ransacked, all his upholstered furniture slashed . . . tiles taken off his kitchen wall . . . even the floorboards were taken up. Among the debris, we found the empty jewellery case. It was positively identified by the jeweller who was robbed as the one that had contained the Rosary. Now, a close friend of O'Leary happens to be one of our snouts, and he told me that old Dermot had confided in him that he was coming into money. Somehow the Rosary was going to be delivered to him — the snout didn't know all the details, but he said that O'Leary then had to keep it safe until he was contacted, given a password when it would be exchanged for a thousand pounds in readies.'

'But that didn't happen.'

Elliott pulled a grim face. 'The plan went wrong, horribly wrong. We believe that the messenger wanted the thousand pounds as well as the Rosary, and O'Leary wouldn't hand it over.'

'You still haven't said what makes you think the Rosary's up here?'

'Well, Michael, we had a bit of luck. There's CCTV concealed on the building of the flats opposite the door to the block of the flats where O'Leary lived. And we were able to get a clear picture of a man entering and leaving who doesn't live there, and is not known by any of the other people who live in the flats. But we were able to blow up a frame from the CCTV and identify him. It was a fitness fanatic called Lee Ellis. He's got a record for robbery with violence, burglary, resisting arrest and a few other bits and pieces. He is now wanted for murder and robbery. His last address was Wormwood Scrubs, but before he went down, he lived up here. He was born in Bromersley. He left twelve years ago to live somewhere in Essex. Now he'll want to lie low, so you know what happens, he'll almost certainly return to familiar territory. Obviously, we want to interview him. Have you seen anything of him up here?'

Elliot handed Angel a copy of the photograph.

Angel looked closely at it.

'Lee Ellis?' he said, rubbing his chin. 'Has he any aliases?'

'Not that we're aware of.'

'He hasn't been through my hands. I would have remembered. But I'll watch out for him.'

'Find him and you'll find the Rosary. But tread warily. He is a very dangerous character.'

Angel wrinkled his nose. He wondered how many more murders there would be before he would be able to find the Rosary and return it to its rightful owner.

Elliott gave Angel a copy of the statement from Julius Henkel taken on his arrival at the scene shortly after the robbery. It included details of the security of the premises plus all the available description of the three robbers, including photographs of James Argyle and Marcia Moore taken from CCTV cameras concealed inside the jeweller's warehouse.

Angel and Elliott agreed to share any new information they might come across in connection with the robbery, and then Elliott took his leave and made for Doncaster to catch the 4.20 p.m. train to King's Cross.

Angel immediately rang Ahmed. 'There's a man with a record called Lee Ellis. I want to know all about him. Look him up on the PNC, print it out and let me have it.'

'Right, sir,' Ahmed said.

Angel was reading through Henkel's statement when there was a knock at the door.

It was DS Carter. He looked up and said, 'Yes, Flora?'

'Can I tell you about that break-in at Vera's gown shop now, sir?' she said.

He pulled a face and said, 'Aye. I suppose so.' He wanted to get it out of the way. He considered that it was extremely trivial when there were murders to solve and an armed robbery to investigate.

He pointed to the chair nearest the desk.

'The shop owner is Mrs Vera Winstone, sir, and she is very steamed up because she thinks we are not taking the robbery seriously. I told her we take all crime seriously and that we hoped very shortly to bring someone to book.'

'You're more optimistic than I am, Flora. I hope you sent her home satisfied.'

'She'll only be satisfied when we find the robber, sir. Better still, when the stolen items are returned in pristine condition.'

'We don't do miracles.'

'She had some very expensive dresses stolen, sir,' she said.

He sniffed. '*Everything* in that shop is expensive.'

'There were two black lace jobs, sir. They were the same dress, but different sizes. One of them was actually on a display model in the window. The thief took that as well. The other dress was on a hanger on a rail inside.'

'Strange that a thief would break into a shop just to steal clothes. And stranger still that he took two the same.'

'Maybe he wanted to make sure he got the right size? Also there was an expensive display model stolen.'

Angel wasn't convinced. He wrinkled his nose.

'They were expensive dresses, sir — models,' Flora said, 'made from Spanish lace. The ticket price on each was £699.'

Angel blinked, then shook his head in disbelief. He was pleased that Mary had never expressed any interest in anything from Madam Vera's for her wardrobe.

Flora said: 'Including the display model, she's putting a claim in to the insurance for £4,200.'

Angel blew out a foot of air then he screwed up his forehead, licked his bottom lip and said, 'The only chap I can think of who might be responsible for such a caper of this sort is a cross-dresser called Luke Buckley, but he's banged up in

Armley.' He looked across the desk at her. 'Have you asked around the station for any likely candidates?'

'Nobody has any suggestions, sir?'

'Well,' he said, 'let's concentrate on the murder.'

The phone rang. He reached out for it. 'Angel.'

It was DS Taylor. 'Just had a phone call from Wetherby, sir. It was the lab technician there . . . about those samples of blood taken from the car park at the back of the King George.'

Angel nodded. His pulse increased slightly. He felt a warm, busy glow in his chest. If the victim was on the DNA database, he might be lucky and be able to determine whose blood it was that they had found splattered on the car park.

'Yes,' he said, 'what about it? Have they got an ID?'

Taylor said: 'The lab technician said that the blood was not from a human, sir.'

Angel's face straightened. 'Not from a human?' he roared.

'He says the blood was from an ungulate, sir.'

Angel's fist tightened round the phone. 'And what the blazes is an ungulate?'

'An animal that has hoofs, sir . . . such as a horse, cattle, deer or a pig.'

Angel sighed. There was nothing helpful there. He shook his head. 'I don't understand that, Don. There hasn't been some sort of a muddle at this end, has there?'

'No, sir. I lifted the samples the way I've always done. I labelled them and sealed them on the spot. If there was a mistake it was not at this end, I'm certain of it.'

Angel had every confidence in Don Taylor. He also had every confidence in the scientists at Wetherby. It would be difficult to apportion blame to any of the very highly skilled and experienced people concerned. That meant another dead end. The sighting of those drops of dried blood had seemed to be the best lead to solving the curious business of the disappearing body, the screwed-down sofa and all the other idiosyncratic mysteries that had occurred in and around the King George Hotel the previous week.

He ended the call and replaced the receiver.

He turned to DS Carter and said, 'The lab says the blood is from a farm animal, Flora. I think somebody is making a fool out of us. It has thrown my thinking completely out of kilter. I need a bit of time to think things out . . .'

'Shall I leave you, sir?' she said. 'I've a lot to catch up on. My reports are way behind.'

He was pleased. He nodded. She smiled and went out.

He leaned back in the swivel chair and looked up at the ceiling. He was thinking about the blood result from Wetherby. An ungulate indeed! But he could not arrive at any logical explanation other than the obvious one, that there must have been a sheep, goat, deer or pig at the rear of the King George Hotel and it must have been wounded or injured, possibly in an accident of some sort, and drops of its blood had dripped onto the ground. He decided to leave the matter there and move on.

He then picked up the copy of Henkel's statement that Mathew Elliott had left with him, re-read it and looked closely at the two photographs included with it. Then he made a decision. He shoved the photographs into his briefcase, put on his coat, and went out of the station to the car.

It was late in the afternoon and a layer of frost was forming everywhere. The BMW slithered its way to the King George Hotel. Angel parked the car out front, grabbed the briefcase, went in through the main entrance, found his way to the reception office and knocked on the door.

When Mrs Fortescue saw her visitor was Angel, she smiled. 'How very nice to see you again, Inspector. Please sit down. What can I do for you?'

'Sorry to bother you again, Mrs Fortescue,' he said. He opened the briefcase and took out the photograph of the woman known as Marcia Moore. 'I want you to look at this and tell me if you recognize this woman.'

Mrs Fortescue held out a hand to take the photograph and eagerly looked at it.

Angel noted the shapely, manicured, suntanned fingers and pink-painted nails. Also, on her wrist she wore a gold bracelet with many charms hanging from it. It rattled at the slightest movement.

'Yes. That's her, Inspector,' she said, eyes shining. 'That's the one.'

'Did she stay in the hotel the night of Wednesday 7th?'

Mrs Fortescue hesitated. 'She did not *book* into the hotel, Inspector, but I can't say for certain that she didn't stay the night, can I? I may be misjudging her, but I mean, she looks the sort that . . . well, you know.'

'Yes, I know,' Angel said. 'But we don't *know* that do we? Is that the woman who came into this office the following morning asking for Mr Domino?'

'Oh yes. That's her,' she said. Then she added, 'Who is she?'

Angel pursed his lips. 'Just somebody we need to speak to,' he said, trying to sound casual. He wasn't going to say that she was a member of the gang who stole the Rosary once owned by Queen Mary I of England. The newspapers and television were full of it and Mrs Fortescue might not be able to contain herself.

'If she turns up again,' he said, 'let me know.'

'I certainly will,' she said.

Angel nodded. He took back the photograph of Marcia Moore and offered her the one of James Argyle. 'Have you seen this man before? Did he stay here that Wednesday night?'

Mrs Fortescue rattled her charm bracelet and took the photograph. She peered at it closely.

Angel watched her, lightly massaging his chin between two fingers and a thumb.

Eventually she said, 'He didn't stay here on Wednesday night, but I do believe I have seen him . . . even spoken to him, recently.' She looked at Angel and said, 'Do you know, I believe he's a Scot, Inspector. If it's the man I think it is he speaks with a Scottish accent.'

Angel's face brightened. There was nothing on the photograph to have given away that information.

'He is certainly from Scotland, Mrs Fortescue,' he said, 'but I don't know about his accent.'

She handed the photograph back to Angel.

'Can you remember where and when you saw him?' he said. 'It could be vitally important.'

'I have seen him . . . spoken to him sometime recently. But I can't be more exact, sorry. He must have asked me a question or I had reason to address him about something.'

'Or maybe you heard him speaking to somebody else? Can you really stretch your memory and pinpoint the time and place?'

'I've done all that, Inspector. I can't. I'm sorry.'

Angel nodded. 'All right, Mrs Fortescue. Thank you very much,' he said as he put the photograph back into his briefcase.

'Is there anything else I can help you with?' she said.

'Yes, as a matter of fact there is . . . there are a couple of points. You said that Mr Domino booked two single rooms and he specifically wanted the penthouse on the top floor.'

'That's right. It's actually a family room, but he wanted it for himself, and he wanted the other room for Mr Memoré to be immediately beneath his.'

'That would be the fourth floor?'

She rattled her bracelet and said, 'Yes.'

Angel lowered his eyebrows. 'Did he say why?'

'No he didn't. It seemed very important to him, so I assured him that I would arrange it.'

'Mmm,' Angel said. He rubbed his chin. 'You had a Mr Wiseman staying here that night as well, where was his room?'

She blinked in surprise. 'I didn't know that you knew Mr Wiseman, Inspector?' she said as she turned back the pages of the huge booking planner.

He didn't reply.

'Mr Wiseman was in room 212, Inspector. He was on the second floor, two floors below Mr Memoré.'

'Was he directly below?'

'Yes, he was,' she said. 'Why?'

'I just wondered.'

She looked at him closely, smiled and in a confidential tone said, 'You know what this is all about, Inspector, don't you?'

'One or two ideas developing, Mrs Fortescue. Nothing definite,' he said.

'I recognize you now,' she said. I thought I knew the name. Never out of the papers. You're that well-known detective . . . that Inspector Angel. The man who always gets his man, like the Mounties, aren't you?'

He gave a slight shrug. He didn't like the celebrity status the media had given him. 'I suppose so,' he said. 'There's just one more thing I'd like to ask you to do for me, Mrs Fortescue.'

Her eyes shone, she leaned forward and said, 'Yes, Inspector, what is it? Do say. Anything. *Anything* at all.'

'Tell me when the hotel's dustbins were last emptied and the rubbish collected?'

Her jaw dropped open. 'Dustbins? . . . Emptied?' she said. She shook her head in surprise. Eventually she said, 'They are scheduled to be emptied every Wednesday morning, early, I understand. Why do you want to know that?'

'Thank you,' he said. He wasn't going to explain. The time matched what Don Taylor had discovered and explained why SOCO was not able to recover any evidence from discarded waste from Domino's and Memoré's rooms.

'Thank you very much, Mrs Fortescue. You've been most helpful.'

'Have I really? It's a pleasure, Inspector Angel,' she said. 'Please feel free to call anytime.'

Angel stood up. 'That's very good of you. There's one more question, before I go, if you don't mind?'

She looked at him and beamed.

'It may sound strange, but I have a good reason for asking, I assure you,' he said. 'Did you have any animals — for whatever reason — in the area at the back of the hotel on Tuesday or Wednesday last week?'

Her face changed. She sat upright in the chair. 'Animals?' she said, her face as scarlet as a judge's robe. 'Whatever do you mean, Inspector? Certainly not. Good gracious me. Occasionally a visitor may have a dog with them and . . .'

'No. I don't mean pets, Mrs Fortescue. I mean cloven-footed animals such as sheep, cows, goats, deer or pigs. Ungulates, I understand is the umbrella term.'

'No, Inspector Angel, we did not. This is a hotel, not a zoo. We do not accommodate ungulates with or without umbrellas. The accommodation is one star rated and is designed for civilized human beings only.' She stood up and crossed to the door. 'I'm sorry, you will have to leave now. I have an important appointment shortly . . . at five o'clock and I have to prepare for it. You will excuse me.'

Angel frowned. He wondered what had happened to her. He noticed that the clock said 4.52. He was tired. It was almost the end of an imperfect day.

'Good afternoon,' she said without conviction.

The door closed behind him.

He returned to the BMW parked on the busy road in front of the King George Hotel to find the windscreen with a layer of frost across it. He looked around at the dark grey and sparkling white scene, with street and shop lights shining out across the pavements, and passing car and bus headlights reflecting the frost as they slithered along.

He got into the car, started the engine, switched on the screen wipers and the lights, and glanced at the dashboard clock. It was 4.55 p.m. He had planned to see Harry Wiseman, but he was greatly tempted to go home. He would have been happy to get the car out of the weather and into his garage but he was also eager to see Wiseman's reaction to the photograph of Marcia Moore.

He was parked only fifty or sixty yards from the Feathers, so he decided to walk that short distance. Accordingly, he switched off the car lights, the wipers and the ignition, reached out for the briefcase and got out of the car.

Five minutes later, he was knocking on room number 202 in the Feathers.

Wiseman opened the door and gave him a welcoming smile. 'Come in, Inspector Angel. And what can I do for you? Oh dear. You look very cold. Here, let me offer you a drink, a whisky perhaps?'

'No, Mr Wiseman. Thank you. I shall only be here a couple of minutes.'

'Well at least sit down. Tell me, have you found the body?'

Angel looked at him thoughtfully, opened the briefcase, produced the photograph of Marcia Moore and offered it to him. 'Have you seen this woman before?' he said.

Wiseman looked at it carefully, holding it in both hands. His mouth dropped open. He looked across at Angel. 'Where did you get this?'

Angel looked back at him deadpan.

Holding the photograph in one hand, Wiseman pointed at it with the other and said, 'That's her. That's the dead woman. Who is she, Inspector? And how did you get this photograph?'

'Are you sure, Mr Wiseman?' Angel said. 'Because I must tell you that later that same morning, a witness told me that that same woman came up to her and spoke to her, and she was very much alive.'

Wiseman shook his head several times, then closed his eyes to think.

Angel waited a few moments then said, 'You told me you only saw the body for a few seconds.'

'That's right,' he said. 'That's right. I suppose if I was on oath, I would have to say that the body I saw was very, very similar. Same mop of blonde hair . . . same clothes . . . same long, slim, bare legs . . . but covered in blood.'

'You wouldn't be able to judge her height, lying down in the alley like that?'

'No, but I was sure it was her.'

'You said there was a lot of blood?'

'It was all over the place. The dress was soaked. It was the same lace dress and coat as this. I *still* think it is the same woman, Inspector, or maybe there are two women who look alike.'

'You mean twins?'

'Could be,' Wiseman said.

Angel wrinkled his nose. He didn't think so. It was a mystery all right. It was a real humdinger. But he'd sorted mysteries out before. It was his business. He really couldn't imagine two lookalike sirens wearing the same clothes being in the same building, one alive and one dead. Someone was lying or mistaken. But why would Harry Wiseman or Mrs Fortescue lie?

Anyway, he could not shake Harry Wiseman's statement so he thanked him for his attention and courtesy, came away, returned to his car and went home.

TEN

It was 8.30 a.m. the following day, Tuesday, December 13, another very cold morning, when Angel drove the BMW along Pine Avenue, through the big gates and up the late Haydn King's drive to the front of the mansion. He kept the engine running to keep him warm while he tapped out SOCO's direct number on his mobile phone.

DS Taylor answered. 'Good morning, sir. I know exactly what you're phoning about. You want to know about that book, *The Interpretation of Dreams.*'

'Spot on, Don.'

'I have it here, sir. Fortunately it was a new book in virtually pristine condition. There were three partial sets of prints. There was Nicholas Fitzroy Meredith, that's that butler chappie, Selina Johnson, the housekeeper, and very clear thumb and first finger prints of one other on the cover which we are unable to identify.'

'Don't those last ones belong to Haydn King?'

'Oh no, sir. His prints are nowhere at all on the book.'

Angel raised his head. His eyes flashed in surprise. In that fact, there was much food for thought. 'Thank you, Don,' he said.

He cancelled the call, put the mobile back in his pocket, got out of the car, walked up the front four stone steps to the door and rang the bell. He was still thinking about the fingerprints when Meredith answered the door.

Angel explained that he wanted to ask him a few questions, whereupon the butler suggested that they retire to the small sitting room which they had used before. This exactly suited Angel's purpose. He sat down in the well-upholstered chair by the fire facing the door, and Meredith sat opposite him.

'There are just a few questions that I need to clarify, Mr Meredith,' Angel began. 'Firstly, that book about dreams, found on Mr King's bedside table. Where did it come from?'

'I really don't know, sir. It just . . . well, it arrived. I noticed it by the side of his bed about a week before he died.'

Angel rubbed his chin. 'He died on the 9th, so you must have seen it about the 1st of the month?'

'Yes, sir. Something like that.'

'And you have no idea where he had bought it from?'

'No idea, sir.'

'There's something else,' he said. 'Mr Fleming had dinner with his uncle the evening before his tragic death, didn't he? Were you present?'

'Indeed I was, sir. I waited at table and served the meal to them both.'

'You could hardly avoid hearing what they were talking about.'

'You are perfectly correct, Inspector, but I am not in the habit of repeating the bits of conversation I may overhear between my employer and his guests, particularly when the guest is a member of the family.'

'Nevertheless in this instance, Mr Meredith, I trust you will break the habit? It *could* have a bearing on your late employer's frame of mind only hours before his death. If I know that, it may assist me in discovering who murdered him.'

Meredith lowered his eyebrows, pursed his lips, rocked his head to one side and then the other and then gave a very slight shrug.

'Yes, sir,' he said. 'You are quite correct. This is an occasion when one should break the rule.'

'I'm glad you agree.'

'Well, the fact is, it was not exactly a pleasant evening.'

Angel's eyelids shot up and then came down quickly. His antenna told him he was about to hear something that might be the key to solving the case.

'Of course I didn't hear every word,' Meredith began. 'I was in and out of the room, taking dirty plates and cutlery to the kitchen and returning with food. And I can say that the ill-tempered argument and squabbling did not greatly interfere with the serious business of demolishing most of a small turkey with the trimmings and a goodly proportion of several tureens of vegetables.

'Mr King was not his usual avuncular self. The disagreement seemed to stem from Mr King having discovered that Mr Fleming had recently seen Miss Savage again, that is to say he had visited her several times since Mr King's divorce and Mr King took the view that Mr Fleming was being grossly disloyal towards him. Mr Fleming's defence was that the visits were purely of a commercial nature. She had all her insurance policies with his company and she needed some special travel insurance for herself for a forthcoming journey to America, also some insurance of some valuable paintings. Mr King took the view that Mr Fleming was not that much in need that he had to go touting for business from his ex-wife. Mr Fleming countered with something about business being frightfully difficult, that Mr King knew about his circumstances, and that Mr King had been holding back from putting *his* insurance business with him for long enough even though — Mr Fleming said — he had bent over backwards to give Mr King the best possible deal. I thought that at that point Mr King was going to throw the cranberry sauce boat at him, but instead, he banged it down on the table and spilled almost half of it, and it does so stain white linen cloths, you know, sir. He called him an "ungrateful little bastard" I believe the phrase was.'

'What happened next?'

'I am not certain, sir. I thought it would be discreet if I left the room, so I went down to the kitchen with the soup dishes and some tureens. When I returned, there was obviously an atmosphere. I don't know what had been said, of course, but they both suddenly seemed to be aware that I was present. They ate in silence, except for asking for more wine.'

'Then what?'

'Unusually, after a small portion of summer pudding, Mr Fleming declined the offer of coffee and brandy, instead he stood up, thanked his uncle for the meal — rather abruptly — and went out of the room. I followed him to the hall to assist him with his overcoat and hat. He didn't make any comment to me about the meal or the weather or anything else. Again, that was unusual. As I opened the front door and bid him a goodnight he merely grunted in reciprocation and dashed off.'

'What about Mr King?' Angel said. 'Was there any subsequent reaction?'

'When I went back into the dining-room, he wasn't there. He had moved to the television lounge with a glass of brandy. I took the coffee pot, his cup and the decanter through. I asked him if he wanted anything else. He asked me if Mr Fleming had gone. I said that he had. He called him — if you will excuse me, sir — "an arrogant little bugger". Then he said he didn't need me anymore that evening, so I said goodnight, cleared the dining-room, set it for breakfast, checked the downstairs windows and doors, and retired to my room.' He sighed and added, 'And that was the last time I saw him alive.'

Angel nodded. 'Yes indeed,' he said, rubbing his chin.

He wondered if the quarrel (and what may have been said afterwards, out of Meredith's hearing) had been really sufficient to provoke Vincent Fleming into murdering his uncle. He was also considering whether Fleming knew the contents of King's will at the time, and perhaps more importantly, whether he was aware of the proposed changes.

'Thank you, Mr Meredith,' Angel said. 'I would like to see Mr Saw if that's possible and then Mrs Johnson.'

'Right, sir. I saw him pop in a few minutes ago. He'll be in Mr King's study if he's still in the house. And I'll have Mrs Johnson standing by.'

Meredith left and closed the door.

A few moments later, Harry Saw knocked, came in carrying a bundle of account books, letters and other office paperwork under his arm. He looked surprised.

'You wanted me, Inspector?' he said, with eyebrows raised.

'Yes. Come in, please,' Angel said. 'Sit down. 'I just need to ask you a few questions.'

'Right,' Saw said. He sat down in a chair opposite him.

'There was a book about dreams on the table at the side of Mr King's bed. It's called *The Interpretation of Dreams* by Sigmund Freud. Do you know how it got there?'

Saw frowned. 'No,' he said. 'I don't know anything about it. I work mostly in his office at the brewery and in his study here. I rarely have reason to go to any other part of the house.'

'Yes, but as his secretary, I thought you might have bought it for him, or at least that you might know where it had come from . . . even that you would know his usual supplier of books.'

'I'm sorry. I don't know anything about it, Inspector.'

Angel blinked. It was an all-encompassing reply that couldn't have been more unhelpful. He moved on.

'The last time we spoke,' he said, 'you told me that Mr King was a man of method.'

Saw nodded. 'That's right, yes.'

'Did he keep a note of appointments, meeting times and so on?'

'Absolutely,' he said, 'most meticulously.' Then Saw's face suddenly brightened. 'As a matter of fact, Inspector, I have his appointments diary here.'

Angel's eyebrows went up.

Saw shuffled through the office bumf he had brought under his arm and pulled out an A4-size plastic covered book. It had the words 'Appointment Diary' embossed in gold on the cover.

He passed it over to Angel. It confirmed what the secretary had said. All the entries were in the same small handwriting. Meeting times, the location, and a telephone number were carefully entered. Angel quickly looked up Tuesday, 6 December. That day it seemed that King had spent the day in his office. There were very few entries.

Angel looked up at Saw. 'I don't see an entry for the appointment he had between Mr King and our Superintendent Harker.'

Saw frowned. 'Oh? When was that?' he said.

Angel pointed at the page. '8 p.m., in the house, here.'

'I don't know anything about that, Inspector. He didn't tell me about the meeting. Most unlike him.'

'Forgive me, Mr Saw, but Mr King wasn't obliged to tell you about the meeting, was he?'

'No, but he always did. So that I knew what was happening. To keep me in the loop, as they say. Also, it is strange, almost unheard of, that he didn't enter it in the diary. What was it about, anyway?'

Angel pursed his lips. 'Did it often happen that he kept something like that from you?'

'It must be the first time in years. I don't understand it. We had a good working relationship. What was the meeting about, Inspector? Do you know?'

'I shouldn't worry about it, Mr Saw.'

But the secretary *was* worried about it. And Angel saw that he was.

Angel thanked him and Saw went out, still shaking his head.

As he closed the door, Angel couldn't help but think that Harry Saw was hiding something from him.

Almost immediately there was a knock at the door.

It was Mrs Johnson the housekeeper.

'You wanted to see me, Inspector?' she said, sitting down in the chair opposite him. 'You want to ask me more questions, I expect. I hope you don't think I had anything to do with Mr King's murder, just because I didn't really get on with him. I mean, the job was all right. The money was good. Well, it needed to be for all the lip I took from him about one thing and another. As long as I did what he said, he was bearable. It was just that he was a stickler for everything being just so. He didn't like change. Everything had to be the same. Once after vacuuming in the little lounge one day, I didn't put his chair back quite where it had been so that he had to move it six inches himself . . . *six inches* . . . he gave me such a rocket the next day. I know how Miss Savage must have felt when she was married to him. He must have driven her daft. Now if I'd been married to him, I wouldn't have stood for all that finickityness, I really wouldn't. I don't blame her divorcing him. I really don't.'

'It's not about that, Mrs Johnson. It's about the cleaning of his bedroom.'

'There's nothing wrong with it, I hope? If there's any dust under the bed, it accumulates like you wouldn't believe. I do it every Friday, when I do all the bedrooms thoroughly. I even get down on bended knees and go round the skirting boards with a duster, and I wash them, rinse them and wipe them off, whenever they need it.'

'No. No. It's about the bedside cabinet. There was a book on there about dreams. What do you know about it?'

'Was there? I don't know anything about it. I never interfere with his papers, letters or books in the house. Them things is private.'

'You didn't know there was a book there about dreams?'

'I never touch his books, I've told you.'

'Your fingerprints were found on it.'

Her jaw dropped. Her eyes flashed in alarm.

Angel could see that she was floundering round for an explanation. 'Ah well,' she said at length. 'I would have to pick it up to dust it, wouldn't I?'

'But you didn't open it?'

'Of course not, Inspector. I told you, such things might be private.'

He licked his bottom lip with the tip of his tongue. 'Well, tell me,' he said. 'How did your prints get onto the pages of the book?'

Her eyes flitted hither and thither, her mind in disarray.

'If I dropped it on the floor, the pages might fall open,' she said, watching him closely. 'I think I remember doing that. Yes, that's what happened.'

Angel shook his head. His lips tightened back against his teeth. 'Your prints were on more than fifteen pages,' he said. 'You must have been reading it.'

Her cocky voice turned into a whine. 'I was only glancing through it, Inspector. To tell the truth it wasn't very interesting. Surely *that's* not a crime.'

'That's not a crime,' he said, staring at her. 'But I'll tell you what *is* a crime, Mrs Johnson.'

He paused. He had her full attention.

'Lying to a police officer when he's asking questions in a murder case,' he said. '*That's* a crime.'

Her face went scarlet. 'Oh,' she said. 'Oh dear.' She didn't know what to say next. 'I'm very sorry, I'm sure. I didn't mean to . . .'

Her voice trailed away.

He shook his head. He wasn't pleased. He stared at her. 'Can we start again?' he said.

She didn't reply.

His jaw muscles tightened. He looked as if the smell of the gravy from the cookhouse at Strangeways had wafted under his nose.

Eventually he spoke. 'I said *can we start again*?'

She swallowed. 'Yes of course,' she said.

'Right. Now, Mrs Johnson, what do you know about the book about dreams on Mr King's bedside cabinet.'

'Nothing, really. I saw it when I last did the bedrooms, when I moved the cabinet and the bed. It wasn't his usual bedtime reading. And I noticed his "Six-shot Sonny Jake" book was moved away.'

'What's a "Six-shot Sonny Jake" book?'

'It's a cowboy book. A western. There're lots of them. He always had a "Sonny Jake" book there. He must have liked them. Relax him before he goes off to sleep, I daresay.'

Angel blinked. He was thoroughly put out by Mrs Johnson. In fact, he was angry, but when he thought of the great man's choice in literature, he couldn't stop himself from an involuntary smile.

It was eleven o'clock when Angel arrived back at the station. He was cold, tired and thoroughly fed up. He slammed the office door, threw his coat at the hook on the side of the stationery cupboard and missed. He pulled a face at it, considered whether to go over and pick it up, decided not to, then slumped down in the chair. He pursed his lips and rubbed his chin. He wasn't satisfied with Harry Saw's evidence, or rather, lack of it. The man didn't seem to know anything about anything.

Angel thought that the evidence in the case collated so far was a hotchpotch of inconsistencies. The source of the book about dreams appeared to be a mystery, but he couldn't see why it should be. Haydn King's prints weren't on it, so it was reasonable to suppose that he hadn't read it. Yet its presence supported the evidence that he was deeply troubled by that repeated nightmare, and it was tragic (and baffling) that that horrible dream had become a reality.

He turned to thinking about Marcia Moore. She was positively identified by two witnesses in Bromersley. One of them was Charles Wiseman, who said that he had seen her dead body in the yard below his hotel window on Wednesday night. However, the body had subsequently vanished. The other witness was Mrs Fortescue, the hotel manager, who had said that Marcia had been to her office, the following Thursday morning. She had spoken to her and she had been very much alive. That simply didn't make sense. Neither of them appeared to be lying. Neither of them had a motive. Or if they had, it was not obvious.

His train of thought was interrupted by a knock at the door.

'Come in,' he called.

It was Ahmed. He was holding a thin, fawn paper file.

'Ah,' Angel said, his face brightening. 'Can you rustle up a cup of tea, lad?'

'Yes, sir,' Ahmed said, 'but can I first tell you first about the query I've got checking out the calls made from Haydn King's home phone?'

Angel saw a gleam of pleasure in the young man's eyes. He eagerly held out a hand for the file of papers. 'What you got, Ahmed?'

'I've highlighted the calls in yellow, sir. Apparently Mr King phoned three times to a place called the Astra Agency.'

'What's that?'

'I've looked it up, sir. It's on Denmark Street. Something to do with show business. He phoned them three times. All on the same day, Wednesday, November 16. Two weeks before he died.'

Angel pursed his lips then slowly blew out a foot of air.

Ahmed said, 'I did phone and the person who answered said that they were agents to the stars. I didn't want them to realize it was a police inquiry so I rang off.'

He nodded. 'Good thinking, lad.'

Ahmed beamed.

'Have you checked his mobile yet?'

'I'm about to start working on it, sir. But that London number doesn't appear on the list, I've already checked it for that.'

'Great stuff. I'll give it a ring now. Hop off and make me a cup of tea.'

Ahmed went out.

Angel reached out for his phone and tapped in the London number.

It was answered promptly. 'The Astra Agency, agents to the stars, Clarissa speaking,' a voice said.

Angel thought the woman had a mid-Atlantic accent and was probably middle-aged. Whether the accent was genuine or affected he wasn't sure.

'Can I speak to whoever deals with Haydn King, please,' Angel said.

'Haydn King, did you say? Won't be a second. Is that Haydn with a hay or a haitch?'

'An aitch,' he said.

'Hold on, please,' she said and he was then treated to a recorded spiel about how great the Astra Agency was and then it went on to list some of their clients and their attributes. The recording stopped abruptly and Clarissa was back. 'You're not on our client base. Are you a producer or a booker?'

'I want to speak to the person who deals with Haydn King,' he said. 'He phoned two weeks ago. My name is Michael Angel. I'm from Bromersley in South Yorkshire.'

She sighed. 'So you're a *new* producer or booker, Michael. I'll put you through to Benny, he's the boss. He likes to speak with new promoters. Hold on, please.'

There was a click, followed by four seconds of very loud rapid drumming and a girl screeching, then, to Angel's relief, the girl died and the woman Clarissa returned.

'Sorry, Benny's on the line talking to Cameron Macintosh,' she said. 'I can't interrupt him, sorry about that. I don't know how long he'll be. Oh, his line is free now. Putting you through.'

A man who sounded like he'd been gargling with petrol and chewing on cheap cigars for forty years said, 'Yeah, hello Michael. Good to hear from you. Benny Astrakhasi, agent to the stars. What sort of a set-up have you got? And who recommended us?'

'Are you the boss, the principal of the agency?'

'Yeah. Sure. I'm both. What's the gig, Bud?'

'I am a police officer investigating a very serious crime and I want to know the nature of the business a man called

Haydn King had with your agency. He phoned your number two weeks ago.'

'The police, eh?' he rasped. 'Haydn King? I don't know no Haydn King. And I would have remembered a fancy name like that whether he was client or a producer. Tell you what, Clarissa might remember.'

'She says she can't recall the name.'

There was a pause.

'Yeah . . . well, if he was selling something, telephone systems, advertising, computer stuff. Dozens of them a day, Bud. I wouldn't know . . .'

'I don't think he would be selling anything.'

'Must be a wrong number . . . we get 'em all the time.'

'It wasn't a wrong number. Three calls were made to this number on Wednesday, the sixteenth. Two in the morning and one in the afternoon. I've got the times and the length of the calls from the phone company. In total they add up to sixteen minutes.'

Astrakhasi said, 'Well he certainly wasn't selling nothing. I wouldn't let him bung up my lines for sixteen minutes with de chat. My phone lines are as valuable to me as my arteries, Bud. I can tell you that. Look, I got to go. I got calls piling up on me. I'm losing valuable business and work for some of de boys and girls.'

Before Angel could reply, his ears were assaulted by drums and more screeching. He pulled a face and held the phone out at arm's length. He was considering cancelling and re-dialling when he heard a woman's voice through the earpiece.

'Michael, are you still there?' Clarissa said. 'If that name comes up, I'll remember. We get more than three hundred calls a day, literally. Sometimes a *lot* more. Give us a bell in a week or so. I gotta go. All the lines are on red. Benny will go mad. I gotta go. Bye-eeeee.'

The line went dead.

Angel slowly replaced the phone. His face was more creased than the prison psychiatrist's joggers. He couldn't for the life of him think what business Haydn King could have had with the Astra Agency, the self-styled agents to the stars, but he was pleased to be out of range of the banging drums and the screeching girl.

There was a knock at the door. It was Ahmed with the tea.

Angel's face brightened. It soured immediately when he saw the bundle of post Ahmed had under his arm. He reached out for it and tossed it onto the desk as Ahmed put the mug of tea on the coaster Angel had set near the phone.

'Ta, lad,' he said as he eagerly reached out for the mug.

Ahmed grinned and went out.

Angel leaned back in the swivel chair and sipped the steaming tea. He was still thinking about the Astra Agency and Haydn King when the phone rang. He stared at it for a time, hoping it would stop. It didn't. Still holding the mug he reached out for it with the other hand. 'Angel,' he said.

'Control Room, sir. DS Clifton.'

'Yes, Bernie. What is it?'

'A report came in earlier this morning that there was a dead man's body seen floating in the canal, sir. I sent Alpha Bravo down. Eventually they managed to fish it out, and the body is now on its way to the mortuary as we speak—'

Angel interrupted him. 'Bernie,' he said, 'Bernie, while I am genuinely very sorry to hear about another poor soul in the drink, why are you bothering me with it?'

'Couple of things, sir. I don't believe the man jumped voluntarily. Firstly, there is nothing in any of his pockets, and secondly, there is a huge wound on the top of his head. Seems to me that it could be murder.'

Angel pursed his lips. That familiar hot buzzing sensation began in his chest, and his heart began to beat louder and faster. Sounded as if the signs of murder were unarguable. But he had such a heavy workload.

'Have you told the super?' Angel said.

'He's busy with the Chief Constable, sir, organizing the Punch and Judy for the kids' Christmas party. He said to get you to deal with it.'

Angel sniffed. He wasn't best pleased. Deep down inside he was angry. He already had too much to do, and he felt that another case on top was an imposition. He sighed. He must stay controlled. There was no cause to shoot the messenger. He breathed evenly in and then out.

'All right, Bernie,' he said. 'Thank you. Get one of the patrolmen in Alpha Bravo to contact me on my mobile ASAP?'

Angel ended the call then quickly tapped in Ahmed's number.

'Ahmed,' he said. 'A body has been pulled out of the canal. I am going to the mortuary to look into it. Ring Don Taylor and ask him to stand by.'

Ahmed swallowed. He was still green enough to be both shocked and distressed by such news, but he was learning not to show it.

'Right, sir.'

ELEVEN

Doctor Mac handed him a white mask and a pair of latex gloves.

'Ta,' Angel said. 'You know I don't know how you can work in this smell all day, Mac.'

'The first twenty years are the worst,' the old doctor said as he made for the mortuary theatre door.

Angel pulled on the second glove with a snap.

'Come on with ye,' Mac said.

A technician in a green overall was swilling down the white-tiled theatre floor with a hose.

Angel followed the doctor across the tiles to a bank of huge refrigerated drawers against the far wall. Mac checked the label on one of them.

'Here he is,' Mac said and then pulled it open.

Frozen air swirled around the body then trickled downwards, hovered around the tiled floor for a few seconds then disappeared.

As it cleared, Angel bent down and looked closely at the fully dressed body of a big man lying on his back with his hands across his chest. His suit and shoes were covered with a thin deposit of grey mud. The skin on his face and hands was a blue-grey colour. The top of his head was markedly misshapen, and his cheeks and chin were covered with several small red cuts.

'That's a terrible-looking wound to the top of the head, Mac,' Angel said.

'It's a wee bit early for me to give you any hard facts, Michael. The body has only been here a few minutes and I haven't had a chance to examine him carefully, but it certainly looks like the blow that killed him.'

Angel nodded. He knew how meticulous the doctor was.

Angel peered down into the big man's face.

'What about all those small lacerations to the face, Mac? By their colour they look as if they were made *after* death. What do you make of them?'

'Aye, the lacerations? There are seven or eight which are certainly post-mortem,' Mac said, then he sighed and shook his head. 'I ken it makes no sense.'

Angel frowned. He had not seen injuries like those before.

A mobile phone rang out.

'That's mine,' Angel said as he reached into his pocket. 'Excuse me, Mac.'

He opened the phone. It was PC Sean Donohue. He was reporting in as directed by DS Clifton. He said that he and PC Cyril Elders had responded to the triple-nine call from the landlord of the Fisherman's Rest, the pub which overlooked the stretch of the canal where the body was found.

'The landlord told us that from an upstairs window he saw what he thought was a man's body, face down among some bulrushes, sir,' Donohue said. 'He went down for a closer look and then made a triple nine. Me and Cyril Elders responded quickly, but we had to call in the Fire Brigade for their assistance. Eventually we got the body out and loaded it into the meat wagon for the mortuary. And that's about it.'

'You will recall the place where the body was seen?'

'Oh yes, sir. We staked it out with sticks and tape.'

'Right,' Angel said. 'I'll send SOCO to take a look. Can you rendezvous with them there in five or ten minutes?'

'I'll be there, sir.'

Angel terminated the call, then tapped in SOCO's number to complete the arrangement. Then he turned back to the doctor.

'I think we've gone as far as we can go, Mac,' he said.

'Aye. I'm sorry I can't tell you more. But I will know all there is to know this time tomorrow, and I'll send you my report by email as usual.'

Angel nodded. 'Thank you for your help, Mac. Would it offend your professional instincts if I were to take this poor man's dabs myself now? Maybe I can find him on the PNC and speed things up a bit?'

The doctor smiled beneath the mask. 'Be my guest, Michael. I'll get you an ink block.'

Angel returned to the police station with a card in his pocket bearing a full set of the dead man's fingerprints. He strode purposefully down the green corridor past CID. Ahmed saw him, jumped up from his seat, snatched a file from his desk, dashed out into the corridor and followed Angel into his office.

'Excuse me, sir,' Ahmed said.

Angel turned round. 'Yes, lad. What's up?'

'Nothing's up, sir. Might even be good news.'

Angel's eyebrows shot up. 'Could do with some of that,' he said as he took off his coat. 'Shut the door, then, and sit down.'

Ahmed took a letter from the Anglian Telephone Company from the file and referred to it as he spoke. 'I've finished checking Mr King's mobile phone calls over the three weeks before his murder, as you instructed, sir. They are mostly calls to members of his staff, his accountant, his solicitor, his tailor, the man who cuts his hair and trims his beard and so on. They seem to be perfectly all right. But then, there are two calls to a Mrs Lin that are . . . well, unexplained.'

Angel dropped his chin onto his chest and lowered his eyebrows. 'And who's Mrs Lin?'

'I don't know exactly, sir. I made an exploratory phone call to her, trying to find out what line of business she is in, but because I wouldn't give my name and address, she wouldn't say.'

Angel's eyebrows went up. 'Really?' he said. He rubbed the lobe of his ear between finger and thumb.

'I didn't want to say I was from the police, sir, so I hung up. But she is in the phone book. She doesn't live far away from where Haydn King lived. His place is that big house in Pine Avenue, isn't it? Well, Mrs Lin's house is round the corner in a cul-de-sac called Pine Close. She lives in number two.'

Angel pulled out an old envelope from his inside pocket and scribbled the address on the back of it, then he looked up. 'When did he make these calls?'

Ahmed looked down at the letter from the telephone company. 'On Thursday 1st December, at 5.10, and then again on Monday 5th December, at 5.17.'

'And did the calls last long?'

'The call on the 1st was four minutes and the one on the 5th was six minutes, sir.'

Angel pursed his lips, his eyes deep in thought.

At length, Ahmed said, 'What does the length of the call tell you, sir?'

'Could indicate whether the call was friendly, or even intimate. An unpleasant call is likely to be short, abrupt . . . and people bickering don't usually want to stay on the phone a moment longer than necessary. Whereas people who like each other are likely to spend more time chatting, making their arrangements or conducting their business, whatever it might be, courteously, happily . . . in no hurry to end the call.'

Ahmed raised his eyebrows thoughtfully, then smiled and nodded.

'All right, lad,' Angel said. 'Leave it with me. I'll look into it. Thank you.' Then he pulled the fingerprint card out of his pocket and handed it to him. 'Check these prints with the CRO straightaway and see if they have a match.'

Ahmed's face brightened. 'Got a suspect, sir?'

'They're from the dead man.'

Ahmed's face promptly changed. He looked at the card as if it had just been fished out of the Pentonville slop bin, and dropped it into the file he was holding.

'By the way, is the super in?' Angel said.

'Yes, sir.'

Angel wrinkled his nose. Then he looked at Ahmed and said, 'Right, lad. Crack on with that, then. And let me know if they come up with anything ASAP.'

Ahmed went out.

Angel sighed. He had to see Superintendent Harker as soon as possible. He didn't want to, but he couldn't put it off any longer.

He needed confirmation that King told the super that he had repeatedly had that awful dream on that particular day. He must confirm the fact before he could confidently take the investigation any further. It was incredible that a man would forecast the manner of his own death and then two days later for it actually to happen.

He went out of his office and up the corridor to Harker's office. At the door, he stopped, sighed and knocked.

'Come in,' the superintendent called.

Angel lowered the handle and went inside.

The old fan heater was still clanking away and the air was sticky from the overbearing heat.

Harker looked up from behind his desk. He had to dodge between the heaped piles of papers, reports, copies of Police Reviews, circulars and boxes of Kleenex and Movicol to be able to see that it was Angel.

'Oh, it's you, lad,' he said with an unwelcoming pouting of the lips.

'Just needed a word, sir.'

'Well, sit down. Sit down. Make it quick, lad. I'm up to my eyes.'

The clinging smell of TCP saturated the air.

Angel said, 'I am worried about the statement you made that Haydn King asked you to see him specifically to tell you about that recurring nightmare, and I wondered—'

Harker's jaw muscles tightened. His face went as white as the lavatory walls in Strangeways. 'Just a moment, Detective Inspector Angel,' he said. 'I have recorded full details of the interview in my deposition. It is correct and complete, and you have a copy. What's the difficulty? Who are *you* to doubt what I say?'

'I just need confirmation, sir, that's all.'

'Confirmation? What's the matter with you, lad? I have had at least ten years more experience than you have, and I am a superintendent and senior to you. Why can't you accept the fact?'

'I do accept the fact, sir.'

Angel saw that Harker's left hand was trembling.

'But you don't accept the fact. You don't accept any facts. That's your trouble. For example, take this Haydn King case, your report clearly states that all the windows and doors in the house were responsibly locked that night and were in sound condition the following morning. So obviously no intruder had entered the place, therefore King's death *must* have been suicide or an accident. But instead of accepting that, which is precisely in line with what I said, and moving on to other cases beckoning your attention, such as finding the Chameleon, recovering that Rosary, unravelling the mystery of the man in the canal, solving the business of the woman's body missing from the back of the King George Hotel, etcetera, etcetera, you have the effrontery to come in here challenging the veracity of my statement.'

'I'm not challenging its veracity, sir. All I want to hear, from your own lips, is confirmation that it *was* the evening of Tuesday 6 December that Haydn King told you about the nightmares he had been experiencing of being found dead, floating in his own swimming pool. That's all.'

Harker rose to his feet. 'Who the hell do you think you are?' he said. Then he suddenly put a hand on his chest and began to look around his desk apparently searching for something. 'I will do nothing of the sort,' he continued. 'Read my deposition. It's all in there. Complete and correct. Now get out. I have a lot to do.'

He began to cough.

Angel hesitated.

The coughing worsened.

He was not sure he should leave him.

Harker looked up. 'Go on,' he spluttered and waved a hand in the direction of the door. 'Get out.'

Angel had no option. He turned, and from behind, he heard the sound of a throat spray being used, followed by a sigh.

He closed the door, stomped down the corridor back to his office, silently swearing. He used every swear word he knew, and there were quite a lot. He slammed the door, slumped into the chair and began to wade through the big pile of papers, files and paperwork that always seemed to be on his desk. He found what he was looking for: a yellow file labelled, 'Copy of Deposition of Detective Superintendent Harker — 9 December 2011'. He opened it and began to scrutinize it. He had to find something wrong, illogical or incongruous somewhere down the line. He pored over it very carefully and slowly. He did this three times. But he could find nothing.

He leaned back in the chair and rubbed his chin.

If the deposition had been anyone else's, Angel might have doubted the truthfulness of it. However, he had known the superintendent all his working life. Horace Harker had been a sergeant at Bromersley when Angel joined as a cadet. He couldn't imagine him putting his career on the line by inventing such a story. And what could possibly have been his motive?

Angel now knew he would have to try to solve Haydn King's murder from a different angle.

The phone rang. Angel reached out for it.

It was Mac. 'I've finished the post-mortem on Haydn King, Michael,' he said.

Angel sensed from the way he spoke that the doctor had something interesting to report.

'Great,' Angel said, 'What have you got?'

'Well, following on your thoughts about the possibility of King being under the influence of drugs, I am sorry to say, Michael, that I found no needle marks on the body, and no sedative or hypnotic drug residues in his blood.'

Angel ran his hand through his hair. 'So you don't think that there were any issues of mind control in this case.'

'I didn't say that. I am just reporting what I found. But you know drugs are not always used to induce a hypnotic state. For instance, stage hypnotists never use them.'

Angel sighed. 'Mmm. You are eliminating some of my options Mac, I hope you realize that.'

'Aye, but I do have something that may prove useful.'

'I need all the help I can get.'

'Well, you will no doubt want to know that the poor man died of a severe injury to the brain caused by a single blow to the head. He was dead before he hit the water. In fact, he was dead at least twenty seconds before he hit the water . . . could have been longer, a lot longer. So, as we thought, I can now say positively that he was murdered.'

Angel was pleased that Mac's findings now confirmed the assumption.

'Thank you, Mac. Anything else? Have you any idea of the weapon used?'

'Oh yes,' he said. There was a sound of triumph in his voice. 'I found minuscule traces of a compound of silica, alumina, lime, iron oxide and magnesia in the skull. The compound was at the deepest point of the wound and would have been deposited there from the weapon at the time of the assault. I use the word "weapon" loosely because it is something unusual.'

'And what's that all add up to?' Angel said.

'I'm not at all sure, Michael,' he said. 'I am still working on it. I can tell you that the wound was V-shaped, because it was made by a weapon with an edge of more than 60 degrees or so. Could be even 90 degrees. The weapon must have been very heavy, or the blow delivered with very great force. I have never come across a wound of this shape. It's not been made by a conventional weapon, that's for sure.'

'We'll find it, Mac.'

'Over the years, I've come across some very strange murder weapons . . . such as a wee candlestick, a boiling pan of chip oil, the leg of a chair, a billiard ball in a sock, the side of a bairn's cot, a sheet of corrugated steel . . . I could go on. I've come across all of those in my time. No. This is something very unusual.'

'Well, thank you, Mac,' Angel said thoughtfully. 'I must find the weapon. I'll have another look round Haydn King's place. There might be something there.'

'Aye,' Mac said. 'Before you do that, I have something else to tell you that you will want to know . . . something perhaps even more critical to solving the case than knowing the murder weapon . . . and even more curious.'

'Well, stop teasing me then, you old haggis-eater, and tell me.'

'When I was transcribing these notes and I came to the cause of death, I realized that the wound on King's head had superficial similarities to that on the body of the man brought in here this morning, so I had the body brought out onto the table. I examined it, and I can confirm that the wound is the same shape — and delivered with approximately the same force. I fished around in the man's brain for anything left by the weapon and found several particles which appear to be the same compound I found in Haydn King's skull.'

Angel was astounded.

'So whoever murdered Haydn King,' he said, 'also murdered the man brought out of the canal.'

'Exactly so.'

Angel's heart began to thump as if it was trying to break out through his shirt. The hot tremor in his stomach spread rapidly up to his chest.

This information was much more important than knowing why and how the poor man had received the cuts to his face.

TWELVE

There was a knock on the door.

'Come in,' Angel called.

It was Ahmed waving a sheet of A4. 'I've had a result from the CRO about the fingerprints of the man pulled out of the canal, sir.'

Angel looked up. He was all ears.

'Records advise that his name was Reuben Paschal, age fifty, sir. Came out of Senford Open Prison in August last. Before that he was in Lincoln. Small-time thief and confidence trickster.'

Angel screwed up his eyebrows. 'Any address?'

'No fixed abode. There is an address. It's his sister's. He was staying with her temporarily.'

'Right. Find Trevor Crisp for me right away. Anything else?'

'Had an email back from the Met, sir. It's a reply to our request to them to check on the addresses of Charles Domino and Joseph Memoré, who were staying at the King George Hotel the night the blonde woman's body disappeared and then re-appeared alive, if you know what I mean. And, as you thought, sir, the addresses were false.'

'Huh. Well, surprise, surprise! Anyway, things are moving a bit now, lad. Ask Don Taylor to come down to see me. I've got to keep all the balls in the air, lad. And I mustn't let anything slip me by.'

'Right, sir,' Ahmed said with a smile. He was thinking that it was highly unlikely that that would happen.

He went out.

Minutes later, Don Taylor came in. He was carrying an A4 loose-leaf file. 'You wanted me, sir? I hope you are not going to bawl me out because we are so far behind with everything?'

Angel knew that he had rather overwhelmed SOCO in the past few days. He was also snowed under with work, so he understood.

'No, Don,' Angel said, 'but investigations have to go on and we have to keep up.'

'Yes, sir. Well, the searches and analyses were all done at the time. It's just that they haven't been collated in sequence, put into good English and written up.'

'That's all right. You can do all that later, maybe, when there isn't as much going on. In the meantime, can you tell me what you found in the rooms on the top floor and on the second floor at the King George Hotel.'

'Both rooms had been cleaned and vacuumed by hotel staff when we arrived there, sir,' Taylor said as he opened the file. 'There were no recent prints in either room.'

Angel nodded and rubbed his chin. 'Anything else?' he said.

'No. The wastepaper baskets had been emptied, and we found nothing out of the ordinary in our vacuuming.'

'What about Haydn King's house?' Angel said. 'Now you were looking for prints that didn't belong to King, Fleming or any member of the staff.'

'We didn't find any prints of strangers, sir, on door-knobs, handles, light switches, push-buttons, ledges and the like. And, as you know, King's bedroom had been thoroughly vacuumed, dusted and polished before we arrived. Even the bed linen had been changed.'

Angel's face muscles tightened. He knew it was true. 'Yes. So you found nothing?'

'We found a tiny amount of red dust in the bottom of the bag after vacuuming King's bedroom. We couldn't identify it though, and it was such an insignificant sample that I didn't think to mention it at the time. But it was unusual.'

'Mmm,' Angel said. He agreed. 'Is it hard or soft?'

'It's hard, sir. Like grit. I have saved it on sticky tape.' He opened the file and put the piece of transparent adhesive tape on the desk on top of a white envelope.

Angel picked it up and held it to the light. Then he dug a thumbnail into it. It was hard, very hard.

'It's like builder's dust. Where did you find it?'

'Under the bed. About twelve inches from the wall.'

Angel agreed it didn't seem significant, but he always wanted to know about anything that could be evidence. 'I can't think what it is, but I'll keep it in mind,' he said as he handed it back.

'I think the only other matter we haven't discussed is about the place where Reuben Paschal was pulled out of the canal earlier this morning.'

Taylor took a memory stick out of his pocket. 'We took a lot of photographs of the area, sir. You can see them on your laptop now if you want to.'

Angel turned round to the table behind him and brought the computer across to the desk and raised the lid. A minute later they were looking at the photographs taken earlier that morning on the laptop monitor.

Taylor clicked the photographs through quickly, stopping sometimes to point out matters of interest.

'The body was snagged in those bulrushes,' Taylor said. 'There was a lager can and a small, plastic tub, floating by his head. That was about all.'

'So he wasn't totally submerged, then?'

'No, sir. When we found him he was partly under water. I don't think he could have moved far from where he was dumped because he was snagged in the bulrushes. There was a fresh bicycle tyre mark in the mud on the bank. Look, there's a better pic of it somewhere. We have taken a mould of it.'

Angel looked thoughtful. 'Good. Although we don't know anybody in this case who has a bicycle.'

They finished reviewing the pics. There was very little reliable evidence from that scene.

Angel wasn't pleased. He wrinkled his nose.

'You didn't want a diver to go in, did you, sir?' Taylor said.

'We don't know what we are looking for lad, do we? Only something associated with him . . . and we wouldn't know if it was.'

There was a knock at the door. 'Come in,' Angel called.

It was Crisp. 'You wanted me, sir?'

Angel's eyes flashed. 'Aye, come in lad,' he said, then he turned back to Taylor. 'I think we've about done, Don, haven't we?'

Taylor nodded, then stood up, made for the door and went out.

Angel looked up at Crisp.

Crisp grinned back at him.

Angel's lips tightened back against his teeth. He shook his head patiently and said, 'Where have you been, lad? I asked Ahmed to find you ages ago.'

'Ah, well, sir,' he began, 'Vera Winstone has been in—'

'Not that woman from Vera's again, that posh dress shop?'

'Yes, sir.'

Angel's fists tightened. 'What's going on?' he said. 'How is it that whenever you are missing there's always a woman involved?'

'I've not been missing, sir.'

'Well it must be half an hour since I asked Ahmed to find you. And that woman is never away from the station. What's the matter with her *now*? Is she chasing *you*, or are *you* chasing her?'

'No, sir. It's not like that. You always say things like that. She wants the robber who broke her shop window and stole that stuff to be caught and all her things returned.'

'Well, perfectly understandable. We *all* want that. Has she come with some new evidence, then?'

His eyebrows dropped. His eyes were almost closed. He hesitated. 'No, sir,' he said. He rubbed his chin. 'No. I think she thinks that the more she pesters us the more likely we are to catch him.'

'Huh. I think she must have taken a fancy to you, lad.'

'No, sir. It's not like that.'

'Well, if you're sure you can tear yourself away from her, I want you to go to Nottingham and interview Reuben Paschal's sister. She's a married woman, so there's no need to wine her, dine her and . . . anything else that might come into your mind. You just have to ask her questions, that's all. We have his record coming from the CRO, so you don't need to ask her about that. What I want you to find out is when she last saw him alive, if he had any plans to go anywhere, who his associates were, particularly since August, when he was released, and what work he managed to get recently, if any. I also want to know where he was living, if he wasn't living with her. Oh yes, and somebody will have to identify his body. She's the obvious one. That's not nice. But you'll have to put that to her. You can get her full name and address from Ahmed. All right?'

Crisp looked at his watch then at Angel and said, 'It's gone two o'clock, sir. I'd better go tomorrow.'

'No,' Angel said. 'It's only an hour and ten minutes on the motorway. You can be there by quarter past three. Bags of time. Go on. Hop it. Tell me all about it in the morning.'

Crisp screwed up his face. He wasn't happy. 'Right, sir,' he said as he went out.

Angel looked across his desk, trying to decide his next priority. These murders were getting too frequent . . . he wondered what was happening out there . . . whatever it was, everything was happening at once.

The phone rang. He glared at it then snatched it up. It was Ahmed.

'What is it, lad,' he said.

'I thought you'd want to know that there have been several calls for you from the *Bromersley Chronicle,* the *Daily Telegraph, The Sun* and ITV news. The switchboard put them through to the CID office because your line was busy. They weren't pleased when I said that your phone was engaged. When I tell them that, they start asking me questions.'

'What do you say?'

'I always say I don't know, sir, which is usually true anyway.'

'That's right. Good lad. What were they asking about?'

'They're mostly asking about Queen Mary's Rosary, sir . . . whether it's been found . . . and about the murder of Haydn King and the other murders . . . and has anybody been charged . . . and so on. And they want to know when you'll be available to speak to them, and if you're having a press conference. The man from the *Telegraph* said that the people are concerned about these matters and are entitled to be told, and he said that there is a definite feeling of fear among some members of the community.'

Angel agreed that facts that *could* be told *should* be told, but he would not have admitted it to the pressmen. And although it was always uncomfortable to know that a murderer was roaming around free, he didn't think that there was any need yet for the public to panic.

He sighed. 'Right, lad. I'll deal with it.'

He replaced the phone, then ran his hand hard across his chin. The current situation in all truth was that he didn't have time to give press conferences and interviews. In any case, he reckoned that his job was to gather information, not dispense it. However, he knew he couldn't hold the media back for ever and that he might soon simply have to *make* the time.

The phone rang yet again. Angel frowned and reached out for it.

It was his friend DI Mathew Elliot from the Antiques and Fine Art squad.

'I must tell you, Michael,' Elliot said. 'I have just heard, and I was sure you would want to know, that the body of James Argyle has just been found in a bedroom at the Rexis Hotel in the West End. He has a stab wound through his heart.'

Angel gasped. This was dreadful and alarming. Another victim of the Chameleon. Angel hardly knew what to say. 'I'm sorry to hear that, Mathew. The Met will be dealing with it, I suppose. Are there any leads?'

'Don't know. I've only just heard.'

'There's one thing certain.'

'What's that?'

'If he had the Rosary, he won't have it now.'

Angel was reading the report and looking at the criminal record of Lee Ellis, fitness freak, extracted from the PNC. It made depressing reading, but was typical of so many small-time thieves, rogues and vagabonds clogging up the prisons. The only recorded employment he ever seemed to have had was as a coaching assistant in a gym. He had had a difficult childhood, his father had walked out when he was five, his mother had had various unsavoury partners, turned to drink, then drugs and prostitution. Her only son was in trouble for assaulting and robbing an elderly woman when he was fifteen, and thereafter followed a string of offences for robbery, assault, and handling amphetamines.

Angel uncovered the interesting fact that Lee Ellis served his last term in prison in Armley in 1999; coincidentally, so did James Argyle.

He had just finished reading the last page when the church clock chimed five. He looked up. Five o'clock. The end of the day. Unusually, he breathed a gentle sigh of relief and began to hum the 'Hallelujah Chorus' as he squared up the papers on his desk.

It had been a tiring day with tedious information coming in thick and fast, but still insufficient for him to be able to point to a murderer or indicate the whereabouts of the Rosary.

He stood up and reached out for his coat.

He was fairly certain that the Chameleon was responsible for the death of James Argyle; the tidy stab wound to the heart from a stiletto indicated that. He thought that the Chameleon was merciless in his (or her) search for the Rosary. He must be the meanest of mean creatures and Angel couldn't wait to get him behind bars.

He fastened the buttons of his coat, switched off the light, closed the door and made his way down the corridor. He licked his lower lip as he pulled up the overcoat collar in anticipation of the cold outside.

It was worrying him that progress in actually detecting the villain was virtually negligible. He hoped he wasn't losing his touch. He sometimes felt that somebody or something was out there anticipating what he intended to do, and putting up obstacles to frustrate him in every move he chose to make. He would love to pack it all in and vanish to the warmth of the Maldives with Mary for a month and let somebody else deal with it all. However, the mortgage had to be paid, and the bills for the gas and electricity were relentless, progressively increasing month over month. He was fed up of running around the house closing windows, switching off lights and turning down thermostats to reduce consumption.

He reached the station cells, said, 'Goodnight,' to the duty jailer and went out through the back door.

It was freezing cold and the moon was already up in a clear black sky. He reached the BMW, pressed the key remote, got into the car, started the engine and switched on the headlights.

He pursed his lips. He would have much preferred to have his own team examine the body of James Argyle and take responsibility for the scene of the crime, but he had to accept that, because of the location, it was entirely a matter for the Met.

He pushed the gearstick forward and let in the clutch. As he turned left out of the yard, there was a flash of bright light in his rear mirror. It persisted and stayed with him for a half a mile until they reached the town centre under the bright yellow halogen streetlights. As he stopped at traffic lights, he saw the reflection of the outline of the car in the glass of a window of a shop that was empty and for sale. The car was a large, black Mercedes driven by a man or a woman with fair hair, with one or more passengers. He smiled very slightly. He had seen it before, several times. He reckoned it would be a stringer with a young reporter from some London national daily, determined to make a name for himself.

The lights changed to green. He let in the clutch and raced forward, hoping to be able to get the car's index number through his rear mirror. The Mercedes quickly closed the gap. Angel knew he would not be able to read it once they were out of the town centre and didn't have the benefit of the streetlights. On the third occasion he managed to read it. At the next set of lights, he took out an old envelope from his inside pocket and wrote the number down. Then he took out his mobile and tapped in the station number. The response thankfully was prompt.

'Operations Room, Bromersley Police.'

He recognized the familiar voice of Sergeant Clifton. 'DI Angel. Bernie, I'm on my way home being followed by a car. Will you do an index check for me and ring me back?'

Clifton grunted then said, 'Better still, sir, do you want me to send a patrol along and sort him out?'

'No. Nothing like that. I expect it's an eager-beaver reporter trying to make a name for himself.'

Angel gave him the number.

The traffic lights changed and the cars moved off.

Angel was determined not to lead the Mercedes to his home. He didn't want Mary being bothered. So he made his way across town onto the ring road and into a housing estate he knew well. It was built in the twenties and the streetlights were very limited. The Mercedes followed thirty or forty yards behind.

His mobile rang. It was Sergeant Clifton. 'That car is a local hire car, sir. Henderson's on Eastgate. I rang them and spoke to Mr Henderson. It's on hire to a chap from London called Dalrymple. Come to think of it, there's a Percy Dalrymple writes for the *Daily Gazette*. Could be him.'

Angel beamed. 'Ah yes. Thanks, Bernie. Goodnight.'

'Goodnight, sir.'

Angel closed the mobile and pushed it back into his pocket. All he had to do then was to lose the Mercedes and go home. He looked in his mirror at the driver with the fair hair. Then he put his foot down on the accelerator, made a few deft turns, then drove into a ginnel, switched off the lights and the engine. He ducked as low as he could in the driving seat, still managing to peer into the offside door mirror. He waited for the Mercedes to pass the ginnel end then he quickly reversed out and went home.

THIRTEEN

It was 8.28 a.m. on Wednesday, 14 December.

Angel arrived at his office with bleary eyes and not at his best. He had not had a good night. He had been awakened at 3.30 a.m. with an idea about the disappearing body of the blonde woman, Marcia Moore, being seen at the rear of the King George Hotel who came back to life six hours later. The idea had been initiated by a news item about a national chain of fashion boutiques being put into administration. It came to him as he was watching *News at Ten* on the television.

He picked up the phone and summoned Ahmed.

'I want you to contact that witness, Harry Wiseman, and make an appointment for him to see me . . . here.' Angel said.

'Right, sir,' Ahmed said.

'And find DS Crisp. I want to see him ASAP.'

'He's here, sir. On his way.'

There was a knock at the door. It was Trevor Crisp.

'Come in, lad,' Angel said. 'Sit down. Tell me. What did you find out?'

'Not a lot, sir.' Crisp said, settling in the chair. 'Apparently Reuben Paschal had been an actor. Shakespeare and all that.'

Angel nodded. 'I knew that. It was on his record. Didn't you read it?'

'Didn't get chance, sir. You said get the address from Ahmed and go.'

'I didn't say, "don't read his record," did I? You can't blame me for leaving without being adequately briefed. You had every opportunity of reading up his record. It would only have taken two or three minutes. Anyway, you can read it now.'

He picked up the phone and tapped in two digits. Ahmed answered.

'You've got Reuben Paschal's file in there, lad,' Angel said. 'Bring it through here.'

'Right, sir,' Ahmed said.

Angel put the phone back in its holster, looked up at Crisp and said, 'It's coming. Now then, what did you find out?'

Crisp pulled a disagreeable face, then said, 'Paschal told his sister that his agent had got him an audition in Bromersley on the 5th of December and if he got the part, he would be away for a few days. Then, apparently on the 6th, he phoned her and was elated that he'd got it. He said that with the earnings he'd be able to afford to get his own flat and not be a nuisance to her and her husband anymore. And that was the last she heard from him.'

Angel nodded. 'Where was he ringing from?'

'From here, sir, Bromersley, she said, but she didn't have an actual address or phone number.'

'Did he give her any indication of the name of the play? Or where the job was, or who her employer was? Did he mention the name of Haydn King?'

'No, sir.'

Angel sighed. He wrinkled his nose.

'Did you find out where he had been employed since coming out of prison in August?'

'He hadn't found any employment. The job here had been the only audition he had been offered. She said he would have travelled anywhere. He was desperate to work. Acting was his life. She said he had phoned his agent, the Astra Agency, two or three times a week, but no work had resulted until this audition turned up.'

Angel nodded. 'Did you make an arrangement for her to ID his body?'

'She said that she would have to talk it over with her husband as to when he could get time off work to drive her up here.'

'Right, lad. I'll leave that with you. Now, what about his recent associates? Who did he mix with?'

'She said that he didn't go out. Not while he was staying with her. He couldn't afford to. He didn't have any associates.'

Angel's face muscles tightened. He licked his bottom lip. 'She didn't say anything about him having a skin complaint . . . anything that would explain all those cuts to his face?'

'To tell the truth, sir, I didn't bring that up. You didn't mention it to me and it never crossed my mind.'

Angel shuffled irritably in the chair.

'Sorry, sir' Crisp said.

Angel gave a little nod. 'Right, lad. You'd better crack on with writing up your report then.'

He got up to go.

There was a knock at the door. 'Come in.'

It was Ahmed, carrying a thin yellow paper file. 'Good morning, sir. Morning, Sergeant.'

'Paschal's file, lad?' Angel said, holding out his hand. He took the file and called out, 'Hang on, Trevor.'

Crisp was almost through the door. He turned back.

'Reuben Paschal's file. Take a look,' Angel said, opening the file.

Ahmed went out and closed the door.

Crisp sat back down in the chair.

At the top of the first page in the file was the caption 'Reuben Paschal.' Immediately underneath were three photographs (one from the front and both profiles) of a big man with a beard. Angel stared at them, blinked then breathed out a long sigh of realization. He turned the file through 180 degrees, pushed it towards Crisp and said, 'Look at that. I have only just realized. Who does *that* remind you of?'

Crisp looked at the prison photographs, lowered his eyebrows and said, 'It's Reuben Paschal, sir. It says so at the top.'

Angel's eyes flashed. 'I know it's Reuben Paschal, lad! That's clear enough. But the photos show him wearing a beard. The body we saw *wasn't* wearing a beard. I'm asking you — *with* the beard, who does it remind you of?'

Crisp looked again at the photographs, then at Angel and then back at the photographs. His jaw dropped. 'Haydn King, sir. Of course!'

'Exactly,' Angel said triumphantly.

Crisp looked at the photographs again. 'We've never seen Paschal with a beard, but I can see that it is him.'

Angel was rubbing his chin. 'Now why would Haydn King want to employ a lookalike?'

Crisp said, 'I don't think that if you knew King at all well, Paschal would be able to pass himself off as him.'

'Mmm. P'raps not close up, but he'd get away with it at a few yards distance, wouldn't he? And he'd certainly fool anybody if he had been in a car.'

Crisp nodded enthusiastically. 'Oh yes, sir.'

Angel continued rubbing his chin, then, with real enthusiasm in his voice said, 'Well, let's have King's chauffeur, Mark Rogers, in for a little chat.'

'I'll get right onto it, sir,' Crisp said and stood up.

The phone rang.

Angel looked at Crisp and said, 'Wait a minute, Trevor.'

He picked up the phone and was greeted by a loud protracted bout of coughing. He held the phone away from his ear and waited.

Crisp looked at him with a questioning expression.

'The super,' Angel mouthed silently.

Eventually he heard a panting voice from the phone: 'Ah, Angel? Are you there?'

'Yes, sir,' Angel said.

'There's a triple nine,' Harker said, 'looks like another murder.'

It was a bombshell, and so soon after the report of finding the body of James Argyle.

Angel's mouth dropped open. He took a small, silent intake of breath.

'A young man. And he has a wound to the heart, possibly caused by a stiletto.' Harker added.

Angel knew instantly it would be the work of the Chameleon.

He felt cold, hollow and empty.

'Who is the victim, sir?' he said.

Crisp looked up when he heard Angel say 'victim'.

'There's no ID,' Harker said. 'The witness said that it is a man . . . a young man. Found in a burnt-out old car up a farm track off Two Pins Lane at the back of Jubilee Park. There's a patrol car standing by and the witness who found it.'

'Right, sir,' Angel said.

'"Right, sir",' Harker said mockingly. 'Is that all you have to say? You are taking this all very calmly, lad. That's six murders in the last three weeks and you haven't charged *one* person. Are you going to allow this villain to slaughter the entire population before doing something?'

Angel's head was buzzing. He didn't have any excuses to offer.

'I have a new line of inquiry that might lead me to an arrest of the murderer of Haydn King,' he said.

'Oh yes? Who's that, then?'

'The chauffeur, Mark Rogers.'

'The chauffeur? Well, er right. If you think it's him, for God's sake charge him, but *do* get on with it. What about this woman, Mrs Lin? What have you made of her?'

'I haven't had the opportunity of seeing her yet, sir.'

'*What*?!' Harker yelled. The cry started him off on another fit of coughing. This continued for a few seconds.

He didn't seem able to stop. Angel heard the click of the receiver as the superintendent's phone hit the cradle.

Angel hesitated. He didn't know whether to hold on or assume the conversation had ended. He waited a moment then banged down the handset. He turned to Crisp and quickly told him about the report of the suspected case of murder and its location.

'It's the Chameleon again, isn't it, sir?' Crisp said.

'Looks very much like it, lad. We've got to catch him. He must be in Bromersley now. He's not far away from us.'

'Have you really no idea who it might be, sir?'

'Now look, lad, forget about King's chauffeur. I'll get Ahmed to deal with it. I want you to start this investigation, without me. There's something else I must do. You know what's to be done. You've seen me do it often enough. Be meticulous. If you ID the victim let me know. Ring me on my mobile. Stay at the scene until I get to you, and tell Don Taylor and Dr Mac I'll be along later. All right?'

Crisp's face brightened. 'Right, sir,' he said and he rushed out.

Angel watched the door close and slowly bit his lower lip. He hoped that he had made a good decision. He reached out for the phone and tapped in the CID room number. It was answered by Ahmed.

'I want you to get me Mark Rogers, lad,' he said. 'He was Haydn King's chauffeur — he might be working for Vincent Fleming now — and ask him to come in and see me here later this afternoon. I'm going out just now. I'll be back in an hour or so.'

Angel replaced the phone, reached out for his coat, went out of the office and charged up the corridor.

Four minutes later he was outside the small double gates of Number 2 Pine Close round the corner from Pine Avenue where Haydn King's and Detective Superintendent Harker's houses were located.

He pulled the BMW close up to the kerb, got out, made his way quickly through the gates, up the short drive to the front door. He mounted the two steps, found a porcelain push-button decorated with a cyclamen flower on the door jamb and pressed it.

While he waited, he looked round at the tidy, symmetrical garden, the shiny black door with its polished brass-coloured knocker, handle and letterbox, and the four potted poinsettias on the steps.

The door was opened by a lady in her forties, wearing a plain black dress. She was strikingly handsome and unmistakably from the Far East.

Angel was clearly surprised. He put on his best Sunday smile. 'Good afternoon,' he said, 'Mrs Lin?'

She looked at him, smiled, raised her eyebrows questioningly.

'I am Mrs Lin,' she said, 'but I don't believe I am expecting you. You haven't an appointment, have you?' She held out a slim manicured hand. 'Have you a letter?'

Angel's smile widened. 'No, Mrs Lin, I haven't an appointment. I haven't a letter. I'm Detective Inspector Angel, and I need to speak to you about the late Haydn King. I am investigating his murder.'

Her face changed. The smile vanished. 'Oh dear,' she said. 'Yes, of course. I had heard that he had died. Please come in.'

She led him into a small sitting room decorated in Oriental style, predominately red and gold.

Angel blinked as he looked round the room.

She pointed to a comfortable chair.

When they were both settled, Angel said, 'Would you please tell me, what your relationship was with Haydn King?'

Mrs Lin said, 'I was very saddened to hear of his death. I got to know him rather well. He had been consulting me for the past two months.'

Angel frowned. 'And what was he consulting you about?'

'I am a psychiatrist, Inspector Angel, and I am not certain that it is appropriate for me to discuss that with you.'

'Well, Mrs Lin, the poor man is dead. He didn't die naturally or peacefully. Don't you think if he could speak to you, and was asked, he would want his murderer caught and punished?'

Her face changed. The comfortable look went. 'He probably would, but he would also prefer the very fact that he was consulting a psychiatrist at all to remain secret. Incidentally, Inspector, how did you find out that Mr King was my patient? He didn't want *anybody* to know. It was supposed to be a closely guarded secret.'

'Does it matter?'

'Mr King was most particular. If it leaked out, he said, certain parties might consider that he was weak and incapable of managing a large public company. He told me that it could even affect the share price of his company. He even swore me to secrecy.'

'I'm a detective, Mrs Lin. It's my job to find things out.'

Her eyes brightened for a second. 'I know,' she said suddenly, with a look of accomplishment. 'It was Meredith, his butler. He told you. Haydn told him everything.'

Angel smiled. 'You have still not told me why he consulted you.'

She shook her head and looked down at the red carpet. Then she looked back up at him and said, 'I am still trying to decide whether the situation requires me to betray my professional code.'

Angel pursed his lips. His face muscles tightened. He looked straight into her eyes and said, 'Don't you want to help me find his killer?'

He stared at her. She stared back at him.

'Don't you see?' he continued. 'You may have some information that might seem innocuous to you but may supply the missing link that could lead to his killer. You must not deny me the opportunity of bringing him to book. Perhaps more importantly to you as his doctor, you must not allow your late patient's murderer to roam around freely and perhaps kill again.'

'You put up a strong argument, Inspector.'

'Well, how would you feel if the murderer were to kill again? It might be quite reasonably claimed that you were responsible because you did not assist me to your utmost when you had the opportunity.'

Mrs Lin blinked, then said, 'Very well, what do you want to know?'

Angel felt his chest relax. He blew out a small breath. 'Did Mr King tell you about the recurring nightmare he had seeing himself floating in his swimming pool, dead?'

Mrs Lin's jaw trembled with anger as she said, 'Certainly not. I would regard that as *extremely* serious. If he had said any such thing I would have been very concerned for him.'

Angel rubbed his chin. 'You are quite sure about this? I thought that that was what he would have come to you about primarily.'

'Positively not,' she said.

Angel licked his bottom lip before he said, 'Do you keep a written record of each consultation?'

'Yes, of course. The consultations are recorded and afterwards my secretary transcribes the tapes, so that a permanent record is kept.'

'How long are your consultations, and how many did Mr King have?'

'The consultations lasted for one hour. He saw me on a Tuesday evening at eight o'clock. From memory, he first came about two months ago, so that would be seven or eight consultations.'

'I would like to see those transcriptions, Mrs Lin.'

'You will treat anything that may be embarrassing for Haydn King with the utmost discretion, Inspector, won't you? And you will not say that he was consulting a psychiatrist? I must try to keep my bond with him even though he has gone.'

'Mrs Lin, I will not deceive you. If I come across any information in those transcripts that I can use to arrest and charge somebody with murder, then I will use it. And if the source has to be declared in open court in the course of delivering the evidence then that will have to be done as well. However, if I find that there is nothing in the transcripts useful to my inquiries, then the content will remain absolutely confidential, and I would probably not even have need to mention that he consulted a psychiatrist at all.'

Angel returned to his office armed with a red pocket file of closely typewritten A4 pages of Haydn King's consultations with Mrs Lin. He could foresee a heavy weekend's work ahead of him. He dumped the file on his desk as Ahmed knocked on the open door behind him and came in.

Angel turned. 'Now lad, what you want?' he said, 'I've no time now. I've got to get out to that murder scene.'

Ahmed's mouth dropped open. 'But he's here, sir,' he said. 'You said you wanted to see him ASAP.'

Angel stared at him. 'Who is here?'

'Mr Wiseman, sir. You asked me to get hold of him ASAP. I've got him. He's outside waiting in the corridor.'

Angel screwed up his face as he considered what to do. He was anxious to get along to Two Pins Lane behind Jubilee Park. At the same time, there were matters he needed to clear up with Harry Wiseman, and the man was outside his door waiting for him.

He made a decision. 'Hang on a minute, lad,' he said.

Ahmed nodded, closed the door and stood by it.

Angel went round the back of the desk, snatched up the phone and tapped in the number of Crisp's mobile.

'Now then, lad, how is it going?' Angel asked. 'Are Don Taylor and his lads and Dr Mac still busy going through their routines?'

'Yes, sir. Did you want to speak to them?'

'No. Have you enough hands there? Sufficient security?'

'Yes, sir. There's all the SOCO team and six uniformed.'

'Have you got the ID of the victim yet?'

'No, sir. We haven't yet reached the stage of being able to search him.'

'What about the car?'

'It's an old banger reported stolen in November.'

'Hmmm. How burned is the victim? Will it affect the ID?'

'Don't think so, sir. The legs and the torso are scorched and partly burned, but the head and face seem to be untouched.'

'Right, Trevor. I'll leave you to it and I'll be down in about half an hour. Tell Don Taylor and the doc to phone me if anything urgent crops up.'

Angel replaced the phone, looked up at Ahmed and said, 'Right lad, show Mr Wiseman in.'

Ahmed's face brightened. 'Yes, sir,' he said.

He turned, opened the office door and said, 'Sorry to keep you waiting, Mr Wiseman.'

The man strode in briskly, his face as straight as a prison bar.

Angel pointed to the chair opposite him. 'Please sit down, Mr Wiseman. Thank you for coming in.'

'I've been waiting in this police station more than half an hour,' Wiseman said. 'You wanted me urgently so I came as soon as I could. I assume it is to tell me that you have found the body of the dead woman?'

'I think we have. About ten hours after you reported the sighting, a woman answering the description you gave returned to the hotel and spoke to the hotel manager.'

'Ridiculous. Obviously, it wasn't the same woman.'

'No it wasn't.'

'Was it her twin sister?'

'It wasn't even a relation. Can I take you back to what you saw that night?'

Wiseman breathed in and out heavily. 'Yes. Yes,' he said.

'You said that you woke in the night, needed some fresh air, so you opened the window and glanced outside. A light shone — you couldn't say where it came from — but it shone briefly on to a dead body on the ground on the car park below.'

'That's right. Yes.'

'You were sleepy. You had just woken up. For how long was that particular spot on the car park illuminated?'

'A couple of seconds or less.'

'Was it a powerful light?'

'No. I don't suppose it was.'

'Mr Wiseman, what you actually saw was a stolen mannequin in a big blonde wig wearing a black lace dress and coat.'

Wiseman quickly inhaled, then breathed out noisily, while shaking his head. His eyes narrowed.

'But there was blood all over,' he said.

'Earlier that day, a butcher in town reported a bucket containing pig's blood was missing. The police lab reports that splashes of blood we found there were from a pig.'

FOURTEEN

Angel drove the BMW along Park Road past Jubilee Park main gate and followed the asphalt road adjacent to the park wall for a half mile to a turning off it called Two Pins Lane, which was an unmade track only really suitable for a farm tractor.

Angel made his way down there until he saw the inevitable blue-and-white tape stretched all the way across the track between a hawthorn bush and a sycamore tree. As he slowed down, a uniformed policeman stepped out from behind the tree, peered down at him behind the wheel, recognized him and threw up a salute, then tapped something into a mobile, looked at the LCD and pressed a button.

Angel drove up to the tape, stopped the car, got out and locked it. He acknowledged the salute and said, 'Everything all right, Constable?'

'Yes, sir,' the PC said. He lifted up the tape for Angel to pass under. 'It's down the lane just round the corner. I've told them you are here.'

'Thank you, lad.'

Angel walked briskly towards the scene.

DS Crisp came rushing round the corner to meet him. 'You're in time to see it in situ, sir. Dr Mac is getting ready to transfer the body into the mortuary wagon.'

'Right,' Angel said, increasing his speed. In cases he was investigating involving unexplained death, he insisted, whenever possible, on seeing the body before it was removed.

As they turned the corner they were immediately drawn into a vortex of activity: patrol car lights flashing; RT chattering; two uniformed policemen heaving the remains of a car door onto a trailer; two firefighters in yellow waterproofs rolling up a hose. And, at the centre, a cluster of SOCO men and women in white overalls, headgear and gloves were huddled under powerful lights over a steaming, smelly, burnt-out carcass of metal, rubber and textiles, which thirteen years ago had been a gleaming Volkswagen Passat car.

Angel and Crisp reached the scene and stopped.

Don Taylor came up to them.

He joined Crisp watching Angel at work.

Angel stood there, his eyes panning across the scene like a video camera, and memorizing everything of significance.

The two front doors and the windscreen of the Passat had been removed, so that Angel had easy and close access to the body. As he leaned into the shell of the car, ever cautious not to touch anything, the rest of the SOCO team and Dr Mac withdrew.

The dead man was in the driving seat, slouched forward over the steering wheel. He was wearing a jacket, dark blue shirt and jeans.

Angel could see that he had a good head of brown hair, pronounced cheekbones, broad shoulders, muscular arms and slim strong hands. The wound in his chest was not clearly visible but he saw a patch of dried blood on his shirt and jeans.

Eventually Angel straightened up, took a pace back and stood there deep in thought.

'Sir,' Taylor said.

'Yes, lad?' Angel said.

'There's not much, sir.'

'Got his ID yet?'

'No, sir. Fortunately his fingers are not damaged. I've sent his prints to be checked by CRO. We might get a match.'

Angel nodded. 'What about the contents of his pockets?'

'That's a funny thing, sir. There aren't any. He's been well and truly shaken down.'

Angel pursed his lips. Now that *was* unusual. 'Whoever did this must have been looking for something . . . something small . . . so they took the lot to be sure not to miss it.'

A small man in white overalls, mask and gloves came over. It was Dr Mac. 'There you are, Michael.'

'What you got, Mac?'

'The wound was made by a slim sharp knife — a stiletto, I'd say — between the ribs straight into the aorta. Placed with the precision of a surgeon. Death would have been instantaneous. He's not been dead long . . . an hour or two at the most.'

Angel remembered how Mathew Elliot had said James Argyle had been found. It was almost certainly the work of the same person, the Chameleon.

'Thanks, Mac,' Angel said. 'Anything else?'

'Aye, well there is,' Mac said. 'Unusually, Michael, the young man appears to be athletically very well set up. Might be a boxer or training for the Olympics, or similar. He's all muscle. There's not an ounce of fat on him.'

Angel looked up. Something was on his mind. His eyes made small, rapid movements. He blinked, then suddenly said, 'Lee Ellis, the body-builder, the lad wanted for the murder of that newspaper vendor in London. I bet it's him. He was thought to have stolen the Rosary from the old newspaper vendor, snapped his neck according to the Met.'

'Could be,' Taylor said, 'How old was he, sir? Do you know?'

'Round about thirty, thirty-five, I think.'

Mac said, 'That fits!'

'Yep. He looks about that,' Taylor added.

Angel nodded and turned to Crisp. 'Check that out online, Trevor. Get a photograph. Quickly.'

Crisp ran to a gap in the hedge into a field where his car was parked. He had a laptop in the boot of his car.

‘Have you seen all you want, Michael?’ Mac said. ‘If so, I’ll get him away the now. I might have more to tell you when I have him on the slab.’

‘Yes, of course. Thanks, Mac,’ Angel said.

The doctor rushed off.

Taylor said, ‘If the victim had the Rosary, sir, that could be the motive for the murder.’

Angel nodded. ‘But the Chameleon didn’t get it. The victim didn’t have it on him. That’s why his pockets were emptied and the contents taken away.’

Taylor nodded in agreement.

Angel pointed to the car and said, ‘I bet there was nothing in the glove compartment either.’

Taylor’s eyebrows shot up. ‘You’re right, sir. Like Mother Hubbard’s cupboard,’ he said.

‘The Chameleon will have taken that stuff and searched through it, hoping for an address or something that would lead him to where the Rosary might be.’

Angel pointed towards the body in the wreck and said, ‘We need to know for a fact whether this is Lee Ellis or not.’

He looked round for Crisp. At the other side of the wrecked car he saw an elderly man with a ruddy complexion wearing a heavy fawn overcoat, brown trilby and wellingtons. The man was surveying the scene and taking everything in.

Angel pointed towards him and said, ‘Who’s that?’

‘He’s the one who phoned this in, sir,’ Taylor said. ‘Claude Eaton. Farmer. He owns all the land round here. The field where we’ve parked our transport is his.’

‘Oh?’ Angel said. Then he went round the car up to him and said, ‘Good afternoon, Mr Eaton. I’m Detective Inspector Angel. I understand that it was you who found this car and made the triple-nine call?’

‘It was a bit of a shock, Inspector. I didn’t know which to ring first, the police, the fire or the ambulance. Looks like the poor chap needed all three! Do you know who it is?’

‘Not yet. Do you live round here?’

Yes. I live in that house over there. In the middle of nowhere.'

'Very nice. Please tell me what you saw.'

'Well, I was shaving, and from my bathroom window I saw smoke billowing over the hedge, so I hurriedly got dressed and came out here, taking a short cut over a gate and across the field. When I saw it was a car with a man in it I wanted to get him out. But I simply couldn't get near the car door because of the heat.'

'If it is any comfort to you, Mr Eaton, he would have been dead. You couldn't have saved him.'

Eaton nodded. 'Thank you . . . that's some comfort.'

'Did you see anybody in a car or on foot anywhere near here?'

'Not at that time, but I did see a big car race past my house about an hour earlier. I thought it was a bit strange. I hadn't seen it before. Obviously he was lost. There isn't much traffic past my house at any time. It doesn't go anywhere. Only to a holiday cottage up the lane. Then it's a dead end. You have to turn round and come back.'

Angel looked at him closely. 'What make was it? What colour was it?'

'I don't know what make it was, but it was big and it was black. I am sure of that.'

Angel could only think of the black Mercedes. He wondered how the press could have been on the scene so early. Then he thought that maybe the car that had been following him had not been hired by a London newspaper, but by others with more ominous intentions. His stomach muscles tightened. It wasn't a pleasant thought. He ran his hand through his hair.

He then saw Crisp hovering close by, carrying his laptop with the lid up. His eyebrows were raised expectantly, trying to get Angel's attention.

Angel turned back to the farmer and said, 'Thank you, Mr Eaton. Thank you very much. Excuse me.'

The man waved and smiled.

Angel walked a few paces away up to Crisp. 'What you got, lad?'

Crisp's eyes shone. 'It's *him,* sir,' he said. 'It's *him.* Aged thirty-two.'

He held the laptop up for Angel to see.

Angel looked at the screen. He agreed. 'Right, lad. Now we know where we are.'

Crisp turned away.

Angel quickly made his way back to the other side of the burnt-out car where the SOCO team had removed the body of Lee Ellis from the car, laid it on a stretcher, and were transferring it to the mortuary van under the supervision of Dr Mac.

Angel was watching them, when out of his eye corner he saw Taylor looking strangely animated on the steps of the SOCO van. He was wiping something small in his hand with a duster. Angel went round the burnt-out car towards him.

'What you got, Don?' he said.

Taylor's eyes were shining. 'A key has turned up, sir,' he said in a confidential tone. 'I was just wiping it clean. See if there were any identification marks on it.'

Angel blinked. His pulse rate surged. 'And are there?'

'No,' he said and he briefly dangled a small key with the number 74 stamped on a round metal disc attached to it by a tiny split ring, and dropped it into Angel's hand.

Angel frowned. He took the key and examined it closely. 'Where's it come from?'

Taylor said, 'It was crudely sewn onto the inside of the victim's jeans near the ankle . . . so that it wouldn't be felt in a pad-down, I suppose. I felt it when I was helping to lift the body out. It was photographed and checked for prints while it was still sewn in. There weren't any discernible marks, only smudges. Dr Mac cut it free from the jeans with a scalpel.'

'Hmm,' Angel said, rubbing his chin. His pulse rate had reached a steady high, and his chest was warm and buzzing with anticipation.

'What do you think it's for, sir?'

'I don't know. We need to find that out quickly. Very quickly.'

He pursed his lips.

He was thinking that Lee Ellis was murdered by the Chameleon for the Rosary, and that the killer had assumed that the victim had had the Rosary on him, and when he couldn't find it, he had emptied Ellis's pockets and taken everything away to search among his possessions for a clue to its whereabouts. But he had missed the key. He wouldn't have expected Ellis to have deposited the Rosary in a safe deposit box or similar and then to have hidden the key by sewing it into his jeans.

Angel therefore thought that there was still a good chance that he could recover the Rosary *and* arrest the Chameleon. It was becoming obvious that the Chameleon was so desperate to possess the jewel that he would kill anybody and everybody who was in his way, so Angel would have to be very careful, very careful indeed.

Angel returned to the office still wondering what that key would fit. He took it out of his pocket and looked at one side and then the other. He pulled open the middle drawer in his desk, fished around and came out with an 8x loupe. He put the glass to his eye and gripped it in the loose skin, enabling him to take a better look at the key. He was convinced that whatever the key fitted would lead him to the Rosary and inevitably to the Chameleon. He must solve the mystery.

There was a knock at the door.

Angel wasn't pleased. It was Ahmed. 'What is it now, lad?'

'Mark Rogers, that chauffeur you asked me to contact, sir . . .'

'Yes, lad. What about him?'

'He's up in reception now, sir. He's come in on spec that you could see him.'

Angel screwed up his face then breathed out noisily.

'I can put him off if you want me to,' Ahmed said.

Angel thought a moment. The time wasn't ideal, but he was anxious to see him.

'All right, Ahmed. That's all right. Show him in.'

'Right, sir,' Ahmed said as he went out.

Angel put the loupe back in the drawer, and the key into his pocket before Ahmed returned with the young man.

'Please sit down, Mr Rogers,' Angel said, pointing to the chair opposite the desk.

'You wanted to see me, Mr Angel? I came straightaway. I want to clear up any queries you might have about my evidence.'

'Thank you. Since then, I have discovered that Mr King employed an actor, Reuben Paschal, who looked very much like him.'

'He was murdered as well, wasn't he? It was in the papers. But he was a crook. He had been inside.'

Angel nodded. 'He was about the same age, the same height, same build, similar beard and hair. I think that this could only have been to impersonate him, or have people, or some particular person, believe that he was in one place when all the time he was in another. It would be particularly evident if the actor, Paschal, had been in a moving car. Now you didn't tell me about this before. What can you tell me about it now?'

Rogers's eyes opened wide like a scared rabbit. 'Nothing, Mr Angel. Nothing at all. Whenever I took Mr King out, it was Mr King. I swear it. Nobody could be quite like Mr King, even if he was the spittin' image. I mean, he always spoke his instructions out sharply, not rudely, but like as if he meant it. And he never said anything that could be misunderstood. You never had to go back and ask him if he meant this, that or the other. And he never used big words or used ten words when three would be enough. I don't think any actor could have fooled me. Nobody could possibly have impersonated Mr King. He might get to look exactly like him, even get the exact voice, but he could never have spoken in the direct way he did. No, Mr Angel, I never drove Reuben Paschal in Mr King's car, I'm certain of it.'

'You're very quiet, Michael,' Mary Angel said as she cleared away the plates from the supper table.

He looked up, gave a little shrug, fumbled in his pocket and pulled out the key that had been cut away from Lee Ellis's jeans and put it on the table.

'Didn't you enjoy the pie?' she said from the kitchen worktop.

'Yes, love. It was great, thank you.'

She opened the fridge. 'Fruit salad with ice cream coming up.'

He nodded and smiled.

'Don't put that dirty key on the clean tablecloth, Michael,' she said.

He snatched it up.

'Are you worrying about something?' she said.

He was thinking about the answer, when she said, 'Is it the gas bill?'

He frowned. 'The gas bill?' he said. 'Why? Has it come?'

Angel hated the gas bill. It was always a struggle to pay it and Christmas was an expensive time.

'No,' she said. 'There wasn't any post for us today. How much ice cream do you want?'

He was still thinking about the horror of the gas bill, when the dish of fruit and ice cream was put in front of him.

'Thank you,' he said and he reached out for the spoon and fork.

Mary sat down. She looked at his dish and said, 'All right?'

'Fine, thank you,' he said through a mouthful of pineapple pieces.

'Well,' she said, 'aren't you going to show me that key?'

He put down the spoon, reached into his pocket and handed it across to her.

She looked at it and said, 'And you think that the Rosary is locked away somewhere. And that this is the key to finding it.'

'Yes, love. I do. And it has to be somewhere safe. And somewhere local, convenient for him to pick up quickly.'

'Mmm. What about a safe deposit box?' Mary said.

Angel pursed his lips. 'But I don't know of a bank or a security firm in Bromersley that offers that kind of service. Our high street banks offer to hold customers' deed boxes securely for a fee, but this key isn't the sort of key that would be used to lock up a small metal box, like a deed box. I think it has to be a key for somewhere else. Also there is a number stamped on the tag. Number 74.'

'Could it be a key to a flat?'

'I don't know of a building in Bromersley that has seventy-four flats,' he said. 'Besides, the key is a bit small for the kind of locks they use on house or flat doors.'

Mary shrugged. 'Well I don't know where else, Michael. You will have to consider the man's interests, his workplace, the sort of places he might visit . . .'

Suddenly Angel beamed. His eyes shone. His pulse began to race again. 'Lee Ellis is a fitness fanatic. It's the key for a locker. Of course. It's the key to a *gym* locker! He's bound to belong to a gym, isn't he? This is the key to his locker. Number 74. I bet that's where the Rosary is hidden right now.'

Mary stared at him her face muscles taut. 'If I had known he was into physical fitness, I could have told you that straightaway. Huh!'

FIFTEEN

The following morning, Angel was in the office early and began phoning the fitness clubs in Bromersley. There were three. He had phoned two and was ringing the third and last.

A man answered. 'Joe Johnson,' he said. 'Johnson's Sports Club.'

'This is Detective Inspector Angel, Bromersley Police. I am making inquiries about—'

The man cut in and said, 'Hey up, did you say Inspector Angel?'

Angel wasn't pleased. 'Yes,' he said.

'You must be that famous one that's in all the papers?' the man said. 'The one that always gets his man? My brother-in-law works for the *Yorkshire Gazette,* and he's told me about you.'

Angel winced. 'I'm not sure about all that, Mr Johnson. I am making inquiries about a man called Lee Ellis. I want to know if he is a member of your club.'

'Dunno. Lee Ellis, did you say? I'd have to look it up. It'll take me a little while.'

Angel lips tightened back against his teeth. 'This is urgent,' he said. 'Important police business. *Very urgent indeed.*'

'Oh. Well, what's his membership number?'

'I don't know.'

'Well, when is his membership up for renewal?'

'I don't know. I don't even know if he's a member. That's what I need to know *urgently*. Also I need to know if your locker system numbers as far as seventy-four?'

'Lee Ellis, wasn't it? It'll take me a few minutes. You've not given me much to go on. You'll have to ring back. Seventy-four? Is that his locker? Yes. We've a hundred and eighty-two lockers here, so his number could easily be seventy-four. Lee Ellis, wasn't it? Lee Ellis. You know, Inspector Angel, that name rings a bell. I'm sure I heard it on the news this morning. Was that the bloke found in a burning car?'

Angel sighed. 'I just need to know if he's a member or not, Mr Johnson. That's all.'

'It'll take me a while, Inspector Angel. Got to go through the membership book. And I'm on my own on reception until the staff come in at nine o'clock. I should ring back about 9.30. I should know then.'

Angel gripped the phone so tight he almost crushed it. Through gritted teeth he said, 'All right. Thank you.'

He slammed the handset into its cradle. His pulse was beating so fast he had a pain in his chest. He had had it before. He would try to ignore it.

He got up from the chair, sent it flying rearward with the back of his knees, pulled open the office door and crossed to the CID office.

Ahmed was at his desk by the door looking studiously at his computer screen.

When he saw Angel he stood up. 'Did you want me, sir?'

'Find DS Crisp. Tell him to ring me on my mobile, pronto. If he isn't around tell DS Carter. I have to go out. Going to Johnson's Sports Club.'

'Right, sir.'

Angel returned to his office, reached out for his coat and began storming his way down the corridor towards the back door. At the end of the corridor he saw Crisp coming towards him.

Crisp smiled and said, 'Good morning, sir.'

'Come with me. We are going down to Johnson's Sports Club.'

As Angel drove onto the gym car park, he noticed the black Mercedes which had been following him the last few days parked near the Sports Club entrance. His face dropped and his pulse began to beat even faster. He drove the BMW into a parking space at the far side of the car park. Then they got out of the car and locked it. Angel then turned to Crisp, quickly pointed across at the Mercedes, said something and gave him the key to his BMW. Crisp pressed the remote to open the boot and began looking for something.

Angel had a quick look inside the Mercedes as he passed it, but saw nothing of interest. He rushed through the automatic door into the reception area of Johnson's Sports Club.

There were about a dozen men and women chattering among themselves who, from their dress, didn't look like members of the gym. Some had reporter-style pads and pens in their hands, others were holding cameras. Angel realized they were newspaper men and women.

As he approached the reception desk, one or two of them recognized him and pounced on him, asking questions about the Rosary, the recent murders, the Chameleon and what he was doing at the gym.

They had obviously been waiting for him. It must have been Joe Johnson courting publicity for the gym.

Angel wasn't pleased. He fended the questions off the best way he knew how. Several lightbulbs flashed as he jostled his way to the reception desk.

He caught the eye of a young lady from behind the counter.

She said, 'Can I help you?'

The reporters crowded round him, as he showed her the locker key with the number tag hanging from it.

He leaned over the counter and whispered, 'Is this key one of yours?'

'Oh,' she said. 'You must be that police inspector what phoned earlier.'

Angel's lips tightened back against his teeth. '*Is this key from one of your lockers?*'

'I think so.'

'Could you direct me to this particular locker, number seventy-four?'

Before she could reply, there was a dull explosion. It came from the basement. The floor shook. A door flew open. The light fittings rattled. There were screams from various directions. A few voices cried out, 'What's that?' There was a loud babble of alarm. Some people ran out of the building.

Angel dashed down the steps towards the source of the blast. People in shorts and trainers charged past him towards the exits. He weaved his way through them against the flow down to the basement floor and along a long corridor. He saw smoke billowing out of a door halfway down. He went through the door into the smoke-filled room. There was the unpleasant smell of burned gelignite.

'Anybody there? Anybody hurt?' he called.

There was no reply.

The nitrate in the air caused him to cough.

The smoke was clearing. He could see wooden lockers fitted on the walls all round the room. Numbers had been stencilled on the doors. There was a locker at the far end without a door. He ran up to it and looked inside. It was black with smoke burns and it was empty. On the floor nearby he saw the charred remains of the wooden locker door. Stencilled on it, he could just make out the number 74. He bit his lip as he sighed. He heard a door nearby banging. He looked round. It was an emergency fire door. It was swinging open and shut in the wind. He dashed through it. The air was clear and cool. It led outside and up some steps. It brought him outside facing the wall of a building. He ran along the side of the wall to the end and discovered that he was on the car park. He was just in time to see the blonde, Marcia Moore, cigarette in mouth, reverse the black Mercedes out of its parking slot at high speed. He ran towards the car and saw the two men, Charles Domino and Joseph Memoré in the back seat. The diminutive figure, Memoré, glanced at Angel, eyes half-open and the corners of his mouth turned mockingly upwards. The car leaped forward into the traffic lane towards the exit.

Angel stopped running. He couldn't have caught them. He gritted his teeth, ran his hand through his hair and looked round for the BMW.

Crisp ran up to him from behind. 'Did they get it, sir?'

'Yes. Let's get after them.'

'Your key, sir,' Crisp said as he thrust the BMW key into his hand.

They ran back towards Angel's car. As they got near they saw that the offside front tyre was flat.

Angel's jaw muscles tightened. He rubbed his chin. He glanced back in time to see the rear of the Mercedes bounce wildly over the last traffic-calming bump and disappear between the exit pillars.

Crisp went round to the nearside of the car and said, 'There's another flat here, sir.'

Angel's lips tightened back against his teeth. He breathed in and out heavily as he reached down into his pocket for his mobile and tapped in a number.

As it rang, he turned to Crisp and said, 'I hope you got that tracer fixed all right.'

'I got it under a wheel arch, sir,' Crisp said. 'It should be fine.'

'Operations Room, Bromersley Police,' said a voice from Angel's mobile.

He quickly reported the robbery of the Rosary from the gym, gave the model and colour of the Mercedes, the licence number and the descriptions of the three passengers. He instructed the duty sergeant to put out a call to all cars to look out for the car and its occupants, and to direct that any sightings of it be reported directly to him on his mobile. Also, he directed that officers were not to approach the vehicle as the passengers were armed and dangerous. He terminated that call and tapped in the direct number to the transport department. He asked for the urgent provision of an unmarked car for his use and mechanics to repair the punctures to his car tyres.

After he closed the phone, he turned to Crisp and said, 'We must look at the tracer screen and see if it is transmitting a signal.'

Angel plugged the tracer monitor into the cigar lighter of the BMW and he and Crisp were soon watching a screen that showed a map of the local area and a flashing white light moving slowly on it. The light indicated that the car was travelling at high speed, much faster than the law permitted, heading on a road due south towards Sheffield.

'Taking a risk keeping on the main road, sir?' Crisp said.

Angel nodded. 'I hope they don't stop and part with the Rosary.'

Crisp frowned. 'What do you mean?'

'Sell it. Pass it on. Hide it. If that light stops flashing — even for only a few seconds — we'll need to note the exact point, got it?'

'Yes, sir.'

Angel suddenly noted a change in the direction of the flashing light. 'They've turned right, off Sheffield Road at the Redhouse. They've turned into a little back road I'm not familiar with . . .' He looked at Crisp.

'I don't know it, sir.'

Angel pursed his lips. He was a worried man.

'Get me Flora Carter on your mobile, Trevor,' Angel said.

Two minutes later, he was speaking to her.

'Flora, drop whatever you're doing. I've got the car of the two armed men who are in possession of the Rosary on a location monitor.'

'I heard your message via the operations room a few minutes ago, sir.'

'Grab Ted Scrivens as your driver. Start out in a southerly direction. When you get two miles out of Bromersley ring me.'

'On my way, sir.'

Angel closed the phone and returned it to Crisp. He looked up from the monitor and said, 'The car's stopped, sir.'

Angel gazed at the screen. He squeezed his lower lip between his teeth and held it there. Eventually he said, 'Where *is* that place, Trevor? There's an inch-to-a-mile map in that glove compartment.'

Crisp opened up the map. 'I'll mark that point, sir.'

Angel didn't take his eyes off the monitor. After another minute, he quickly ran his hand through his hair and bawled, *'They're still there!* What are they doing? Whatever they're up to, I only hope they haven't parted with that Rosary.'

'Looks like a cluster of trees. A sort of mini forest. Look, they're off again, sir. One of them might have needed to spend a penny.'

Angel nodded. He looked at his watch. 'They were at a standstill there for two and a half minutes,' he said. 'That's long enough to have made an exchange.' He looked out of the windscreen towards the exit road then banged his hands hard on the steering wheel. 'It's time the garage brought that car. We can't sit here all day.'

A few minutes later, a replacement police car was delivered to the gym car park. It was an unmarked Ford Mondeo, and Angel and Crisp quickly made the transfer.

'You drive,' Angel said. 'I'll keep my eye on the monitor. Make for Barnsley then Ecclesfield, that would be the most direct route to where they are now.'

Crisp took the wheel and pointed the car towards the car-park exit.

After a few moments, Angel frowned and said, 'They've taken another right. They are travelling north now, towards Tunistone.'

'They're making sure that nobody's following them,' Crisp said as he applied the Mondeo's brakes at the car-park exit. He turned left on Barnsley Road.

'Never mind Eccclesfield, Trevor. Continue to Barnsley, but go through the centre, along Dodworth Road and out in the general direction of the A628 towards Manchester. That should put us in a good position depending on where they are headed.'

Angel's mobile rang.

It was Flora Carter. 'I have Ted Scrivens with me, sir,' she said, 'and we're two miles out of Bromersley travelling south.'

'Right,' Angel said. 'Now, the Mercedes stopped at a place, 1.1 mile east of the Redhouse. I want you to check it out. You'll have to inspect both sides of the road. I need to know *why* they stopped. See what there is and let me know. It's possible that they met the Chameleon there by arrangement and made the exchange. See if you can see anything, anything at all. And let me know ASAP. All right?'

'Right, sir,' Flora Carter said.

'One more thing,' Angel said.

'Yes, sir?'

Slowly and deliberately, he said, 'I want you to be careful, Flora. *Very careful.* We don't know the identity of the Chameleon. It could be anybody, male or female. It could be somebody we know well. So don't venture into situations on your own. Stick close to Ted Scrivens and tell him to stick close to you. All right?'

She hesitated, swallowed and said, 'Right, sir.'

Angel pocketed the mobile and pursed his lips. He was glad Scrivens was accompanying her. He was intelligent. He was also tall and muscular, and would be useful in case of trouble. However, he would need to be especially slick to protect himself against a stiletto . . . well, everybody would. A stiletto was a particularly evil weapon that could be skilfully used to kill by a man or a woman. The Chameleon didn't need strength to kill, simply a little knowledge of anatomy.

Angel returned to watching the tracer screen.

During the next thirty minutes, the Mercedes made a circuitous route in a north-westerly direction to the small farming town of Tunistone, ten miles west of Bromersley, several hundred feet higher up the Pennines.

The Mondeo was by now only three miles behind the Mercedes so Angel knew he could be on to them very quickly if necessary.

The flashing light showed that the car was making its way at a measured pace to the far western perimeter of the town to an estate of council flats. It indicated that the car made a right turn into the estate along a road shown as Marion Road and then first right again into a cul-de-sac named Little John Road. It travelled up that road a little way then stopped.

Angel watched the flashing light carefully. 'I think they might have reached their destination,' he said.

He checked the time then watched the monitor closely for exactly two minutes, then said, 'Yes. It looks like it. They've certainly given us a run around.'

'How near do you want me to take us, sir?'

'Well, we don't want them to spot us, but we do need to pinpoint exactly where they are.'

Angel directed Crisp through Tunistone to the estate.

It comprised a large number of flats built in blocks of four, two above two, with outside separate stone steps leading to the 'front' doors of the upstairs flats. There were very few people in the streets around. Many people were at work or school. The dull cold weather was keeping any other residents inside in the warm.

'This is Marion Road, Ted,' Angel said. 'It cuts straight through the estate. Now drive along here fairly quickly, just as if we are just passing through and we know exactly where we are going. The Merc actually took the first on the right, which is Little John Road and stopped only a little way up. So have a peek up there.'

'Right, sir,' Crisp said. 'Here we go.'

Crisp took the corner and turned into Marion Road.

As the Mondeo travelled across the end of Little John Road, the two men glanced up it.

'There're two of them, there, sir,' Crisp said.

They saw the immaculate and tiny Memoré on the nearest side of the car and Marcia Graham's unmistakable head of straw-coloured blonde hair and shapely figure on the far side. The two were energetically pulling a reluctant grey canvas tarpaulin over the roof of the Mercedes which was parked on the flagstone surround close to one of the staircases of an upstairs flat.

Angel saw them out of his eye corner. His jaw muscles tightened. 'Right, lad,' he said. 'Let's get out of here.'

Crisp put his foot gently down on the accelerator and they were soon out of sight.

'Flat 2, Little John Road,' Angel said. 'That's the address then.'

Crisp drove the Mondeo further along Marion Road into the heart of the estate, made a couple of turns then pulled up at the side of the road.

Meanwhile Angel was speaking to an old friend Detective Inspector Waldo White on his mobile. He was the officer in charge of the FSU, the Firearms Special Unit, in Wakefield. It was a special group of policemen and women on call 24/7 specially authorized to carry firearms and trained to deal with all circumstances where an armed person or persons were behaving in a dangerous manner.

Angel told White the situation in brief and they arranged to rendezvous at the top of Marion Road, Tunistone, in about forty minutes. Angel was about to tap in another number when the mobile vibrated and rang out as he was holding it.

It was Flora Carter. His eyebrows shot up. He quickly pressed the button.

'Yes, Flora,' he said. 'What you got?'

'It's not good, sir. Found the body of a man hidden behind a stone wall . . . just off the road. It's Charles Domino.'

'Charles Domino?' he said. His face tightened, he shook his head, then blew out a lungful of air. 'Stabbed in the heart, I expect?'

'Yes, sir,' Flora said.

'Any signs of a struggle?' he said, rubbing his chin.

'No, sir,' she said.

'Are you sure?'

'Positive. Ted and I have had a good look round and we can find absolutely nothing. There's really nothing here. Only trees and bushes and grass.'

'Any tyre marks or footprints?'

'No, sir. We have not seen a single footprint, a weapon nor anything else that could be a clue.'

'What about the ground? Now, this is important, Flora,' he said heavily. 'This is *really* important. Is the ground round there hard or soft?'

'Pretty soft, sir. There were heavy showers here throughout last night.'

'Any puddles?'

'No. No puddles.'

Angel breathed out noisily. He lowered his eyebrows as he mulled over the information. He reached a conclusion.

Flora said, 'Are you still there, sir?'

'Well, I want you here in Tunistone urgently, Flora, so get yourself to the top of Marion Road ASAP. It's just off the ring road to Manchester. Look out for my silver Ford Mondeo. Now let me speak to Ted Scrivens.'

The young man came on the line. 'Scrivens, sir.'

'Now listen up, lad. I've got my hands full here, so I want you to ring Don Taylor in the SOCO office, and Dr Mac at the mortuary, report that you have a body. Tell them that you've spoken to me and that I've instructed you to ask them to do the necessary. Then ring the super and tell him about the body, and what's happening. Then I want you to stay there and be "continuation officer" because I need Sergeant Carter with me here. All right?'

Scriven's voice brightened. He liked the unexpected responsibility. 'Yes, sir,' he said.

Angel ended the call and tapped in a number.

Crisp said, 'Charles Domino dead, sir?'

'Yes, lad,' he said rubbing his chin.

‘That would be the Chameleon again?’

‘I am very much afraid that it was, lad. Aye.’

‘Do you think, sir, that they met him there by arrangement, and that he stabbed Domino as he was handing the Rosary over?’

‘No. It’s becoming a bit clearer now that he has gone.’

Crisp frowned. It wasn’t clear to him.

A familiar voice answered Angel’s mobile. ‘Control Room, Bromersley Police. Duty Sergeant Clifton.’

‘DI Angel, Bernie. I’m on a surveillance job out at the top of Marion Road, Tunistone. A man and a woman. The man is known to be armed with a handgun. Now, I need a damned good negotiator to talk them out. Who have we got?’

‘There’s nobody at present on attachment, sir. Barney the Brains left, if you remember. There’ll be somebody on the West Yorkshire force, I expect. I’ll contact them if you like and let you know.’

Angel wrinkled his nose and groaned. ‘There’s isn’t time for that rigmarole. If these villains start on the move, we’ll not be able to stop them, and we might lose them. There’s only Trevor Crisp and me here at the moment.’

Sergeant Clifton hesitated, then said, ‘Well, what do you want me to do, sir?’

‘Leave it with me, Bernie. There’s something else. I very urgently need a pair of walkie-talkies complete with fresh batteries from the stores. Send them by a plain-clothes man, in an unmarked car with a squib up his backside, will you?’

Clifton smiled, ‘Right, sir.’

Angel closed the phone.

Crisp said, ‘Who is going to be the negotiator, sir?’

‘Dunno,’ he growled. ‘Huh. Would you believe it? We still haven’t got an experienced negotiator at Bromersley.’

‘But you’ve done the course, sir, haven’t you?’

‘Yeah’ he said. The corners of his mouth turned downwards. He shook his head. ‘Trouble is, it assumed all villains are out of the same pot and they aren’t.’

He dropped the mobile in his pocket and turned back to Crisp. 'It's time we had a look at 'em. See if they're settled in. Get out and amble down the road. See if everything is quiet and keep going. I'll drive round to the other side of the estate and pick you up.'

Crisp got out of the Mondeo, leaned over to the back seat for his overcoat, put it on and set off.

Angel looked around. It was cold and cloudy, and the streets were very quiet. The occasional car or delivery van passed by but that was all. They had seen an elderly man walking a dog and a woman lugging her shopping home.

Angel got into the driving seat, set off up the hill, drove round the outside of the estate and two minutes later, turned the Mondeo into the bottom of Marion Road, where he saw Crisp in a black overcoat walking on the pavement towards him. When he reached him he stopped.

Crisp opened the car door. 'They're on the move, sir,' he said as he got in.

'*What*?' Angel roared. That was the last thing he wanted to hear. His pulse began to thump. He could feel the beat on his eardrums. He shoved the gear stick into first and let in the clutch.

SIXTEEN

'They're up to something, sir,' Crisp said. 'I caught sight of Joseph Memoré humping a big suitcase and a carrier bag down the outside steps. The tarpaulin had been partly removed from the car so that they could load the boot and the back of the car. It still covers the number plate and the bonnet.'

Angel pulled a face; it was a very worrying time. He drove the BMW resolutely up Marion Road. He was deep in thought. He believed Memoré had a small handgun, probably a Beretta, which was just as dangerous at close quarters as the Glock G17, the standard police-issue weapon, was at thirty yards. He also knew that if he allowed Memoré and Marcia Moore to escape from that flat, he might never be able to catch them again, and the beautiful historic Mary I gold, diamond and ruby Rosary might disappear forever. He checked his watch. It was almost noon. He reckoned that Waldo White and his unit from the FSU would still be about fifteen minutes away, so he only had to stall the villains that length of time. Flora Carter would take longer, as would the man bringing the walkie-talkies from Bromersley.

The situation required bold action.

He drove the Mondeo up Marion Road, turned it through 180 degrees at the top and then drove it down again.

He decided to risk taking a longer, more thorough look at the exterior of the villains' flat. He drove down Marion Road and turned into Little John Road. He saw that the Mercedes had been partially uncovered, as Crisp had said, but there were no signs of Memoré or Moore. He drove on for a further 25 yards only, then stopped at the side of the road and pulled on the handbrake.

'What are you going to do, sir?' Crisp said.

'We've got to keep them there until the FSU arrive, which means that we have to set up communications with them *now*.'

Crisp shook his head. 'The walkie-talkies won't be here for another half hour or so.'

'They could be even longer,' Angel said and rubbed the lobe of his ear between finger and thumb. Then he suddenly said. 'Give me your mobile.'

Crisp stared at him. 'What for?'

'Give me your mobile, lad. Come on. Don't waste time.'

'But, sir,' he said.

Angel glared at him and nodded his head meaningfully.

Crisp pulled a face, dug into his pocket and slowly passed it over.

Angel snatched it from him, held it up and said, 'Now listen, lad, I'm going to get out and look in the boot to find something to wrap round this phone. Then I'm going to deliver it to Flat 2, Little John Road, and I want you to—'

Crisp's jaw dropped. His eyes opened wide. 'You can't do *that,* sir. He's armed. He knows who you are. If you go anywhere near there, he'll kill you.'

Angel shook his head impatiently. 'No he won't. He won't get chance. Now, listen. I want you to wait one minute exactly and then turn round and drive to the end of the street and pick me up, all right?'

Crisp shook his head as Angel spoke. He didn't want to do it.

Angel got out of the Mondeo, went round to the boot, from a packet took out a couple of self-seal polythene bags with the word EVIDENCE printed in big letters in red across them, wrapped them round the mobile, pushed the bundle inside another bag, and sealed it. Then he walked quickly back along Marion Road, turned left up Little John Road, across the asphalt area, ran up the steps of Flat 2 to the front door. He pushed the package through the letterbox, turned quickly round, and returned to the corner of the street where he had arranged to be collected and was relieved to see Crisp arrive in the Mondeo right on time.

Angel got in the car.

Crisp let in the clutch and drove away. 'Everything all right, sir?'

'You were a bit late.'

'You said a minute, sir.'

'Take us up to the top of the street and park up there somewhere,' he said as he took out his own mobile and tapped in the number of the other one.

He rubbed his chin as he heard it ring out. He must talk to Memoré and try to keep him and Marcia Moore contained otherwise the situation could end in a shoot-out and a possible bloodbath. There were the neighbours in the same block, people in the other flats close at hand and passers-by who could be caught in crossfire, and they had to be taken into consideration and protected.

Suddenly the distinctive voice of Joseph Memoré said, ''Allo. 'Allo. What is this? Who is there?'

Angel put on his most robust voice. 'Good afternoon, Mr Memoré. This is Detective Inspector Angel, Bromersley Police.'

Angel heard him gasp.

There was a pause and then Memoré said, 'Oh. What's dis? What's dis, "Good afternoon"? What you vant, Angel?'

'I want to tell you that you are surrounded by armed police officers and I want you to throw your weapons out of the window.'

'Nossing doing. I don't believe you. If you want me, come in and get me.'

'We don't want to do that, Mr Memoré. It may result in injury to you and to Miss Moore. Also, neighbours and passers-by may be caught in any crossfire. It would be much safer if you were to surrender peacefully. It would also go in your favour when you go to court.'

'Huh. I am not going to any court. Hold on a minute.'

'I'll hold,' Angel said.

Memoré had his hand over the mouthpiece of the phone, which he removed very briefly from time to time and Angel could hear both Memoré's and Marcia Moore's whispered voices, but he couldn't make out what either of them was saying.

Crisp said, 'What's happening?'

Angel mimed to him not to speak.

After a minute or two, Memoré came back and said, 'Are you there, Angel? I am not going to any court. I am going to get out of here. Anybody who approaches the flat vill be shot. I am armed. There is plenty of food. I can hold out for days. Marcia Moore is my prisoner. I want a helicopter, a pilot and a full tank of fuel. I want that by four o'clock or she vill be shot. Have you got that?'

All Angel's facial muscles tightened. He had wanted to avoid confrontation. An ultimatum was the last thing he needed.

'That would take a bit of organizing, Mr Memoré,' he said.

'Right, you'd better get on vis it, then,' he said.

Angel needed time to think out his next move. He had managed to achieve a delay of a few minutes, which was good. But he hadn't taken into account that Memoré could be so evil.

'I'll phone you back in a few minutes, Mr Memoré.'

'Orl right,' Memoré said. 'Don't be too long,' he added and the line went dead.

Angel shook his head and looked down at his feet.

'What's happening, sir?' Crisp said.

'He wants a helicopter, a pilot and plenty of fuel or else he'll kill Marcia Moore.'

'Oh my God,' Crisp said. 'Where on earth are you going to get a helicopter with a pilot willing to take him?'

'I'm not. He's not going anywhere, and certainly not in a helicopter.'

'Did he believe you when you said you had the place surrounded?'

'He was stunned that we knew they were there at all. He'll believe it for a while, anyhow. He wouldn't think that I would have announced our presence if there were just the two of us and neither of us was armed. The FSU lads should be here in a few minutes.'

'Well, what are you going to do, sir?'

'I'm thinking about it.'

Angel picked up the mobile and tapped in the number. It was soon answered. 'I've got my sergeant searching around for a helicopter and pilot for you—'

'It had better not take long.'

'He's doing his best, Mr Memoré. He's only just started. He's in touch with the RAF at Leconfield, who have several Sea King helicopters. However, he'll probably have difficulty getting authorization for the flight.'

Memoré came back fuming. 'I *have* to have a helicopter. You have to get on with it. Time is running short. There are nearer ones than those. There are the AA and the weather people. They have helicopters. I don't care where you get it from.'

'I'll push my sergeant along those lines if we can't get authorization from Leconfield, and I'll ring you back again in a minute or two.'

'Orl right,' Memoré said and the phone went dead.

Angel looked at Crisp and said, 'Where the hell are those FSU men? See if you can see them anywhere, Trevor. I can't keep these two bottled up forever.'

Crisp got out of the car. He was met by a cold breeze. He walked along the top road and stood around, hands in pockets, collar up. There was no sign of the FSU Range Rovers. However, an unmarked car with a number plate he did recognize drove into view. It was Flora Carter. She flashed her lights, he acknowledged her with a wave and she stopped by him.

'The Inspector will be pleased to see you,' he said.

'Everything all right?'

His face showed that it wasn't.

'What's happened?'

He quickly told her the situation and explained why he was standing there.

'What's the boss going to do?' she said.

'Don't know. He's just playing for time.'

'Better check in.'

Crisp pointed to the turning off to Marion Road. 'He's just round the corner . . . parked up in a Mondeo.'

She drove off and parked behind the Ford.

Angel was thinking about his next move. He saw Flora arrive through the rear mirror. He was pleased about that. She showed her face at his window and he signalled for her to get in the front seat.

'You left Ted Scrivens all right, Flora?'

She nodded. 'He'll manage until Don Taylor arrives,' she said, settling in the seat. 'I was thinking, sir. Maybe Domino and Memoré set up a meeting with the Chameleon there to exchange the Rosary for a bundle of money, but the Chameleon got the better of them, killed Domino to make his escape and took the Rosary.'

'You're half-right, Flora.'

'But who is the Chameleon?'

'Did you see Trevor Crisp on the top road?'

'Yes, sir. He brought me up to date. You're having quite a day. He said that you're managing to hold the two villains at bay.'

Angel sighed. 'Aye. So far so good. But they won't stay in there forever. They've at least one handgun, and, until the FSU arrive, we've nothing but bluff.'

The mobile rang. Angel answered it. It was Memoré.

'Where's dat frigging helicopter?'

Angel pulled a face. He had to think quickly. 'We are still waiting for authorization for the flight. I have spoken to the Wing Commander up there, he says he can't authorize the flight because it is not for the transport of a sick or injured person over an agreed route.'

Angel could hear Memoré breathing heavily. 'I don't give a frigging damn for your Ving Commander,' he bawled. 'There'll be plenty of sick, injured and dead persons round here starting with this Marcia Moore, if I don't see a helicopter here by four o'clock. There are plenty of osser people with helicopters. I warn you if a helicopter is not here by four o'clock, I will keel her.'

Angel glanced at his watch. It was four minutes to four. He licked his bottom lip. 'My sergeant is working hard at it, Mr Memoré. But please be patient. However, I don't think it will be possible to have it here for four.'

'You had better. Her death vill be on your conscience.'

'No it won't. And you have to be reasonable. You realize that another murder by you will make your sentence even longer.'

'You'll never catch me, Angel. You have four minutes to get me that helicopter.'

The line went dead.

Angel ran his hand through his hair. He began to breathe more rapidly. He closed the phone. He saw Flora looking at him. She looked anxious.

'He's all bullets and brilliantine,' he said, trying to be optimistic.

But she was not fooled. 'What's he say?'

'He's still threatening to shoot Marcia Moore if a helicopter isn't here by four o'clock.'

Flora's mouth dropped open in disbelief. 'Oh, sir,' she said and shook her head.

'I can't see what more I can do,' Angel said.

The mobile phone rang out again.

'Angel,' Memoré said. 'It's two minutes to four. Where is the helicopter that is going to take me away from all dis?'

'We have managed to get in touch with a privately owned chopper. But he wants £500 cash up front before he'll even turn out. We're trying to get someone to finance us temporarily, but it is taking a lot of setting up. The banks want security.'

'But it vill not be here at four, will it?' Memoré said obstinately.

'It will be here just as soon as we can get the five hundred and then get the money to him,' Angel said.

Memoré didn't speak. The phone suddenly went dead.

Angel bit his lip. 'He's going to shoot her. He's going to carry out his threat. What can I do?'

He looked at his watch. The second hand was climbing up to twelve. He leaped out of the car and looked in the direction of Flat 2, Little John Road.

There was a gunshot. It echoed round the houses.

'Oh, God,' Flora said.

Angel began to run towards the flat. He called back, 'You stay there.'

'Be careful, sir,' Flora called.

As Angel reached the drive of that block of flats, he saw Marcia Moore running frantically down the steps, screaming and crying, with her hands in the air. She was wearing that black lace dress, but no coat. He stopped and watched her. She didn't see him at first and apparently intended running blindly ahead.

Then she saw Angel, turned and rushed up to him, 'He tried to shoot me,' she cried. Then she put her arms round him, one over his shoulder, the other under his arm. Her whole body was shaking.

Angel stood there like a hat-stand. He untangled an arm and managed to reach into his pocket.

'I got my chance,' she said. 'I had to save myself. It was him or me. It was awful, dreadful. I think he is dead.'

'Where's the gun?' he said as he pulled something out of his pocket.

'I dunno. I dunno. It must be up there somewhere.'

Angel managed to click the catch of one cuff on Marcia Moore's wrist and then reached out for the other. When she realized what he was doing, she pulled away.

'What's this?' she said brusquely.

Angel stared at her. The crying ceased. The tears dried up. The shaking had stopped. She yanked the anchored wrist with the handcuffs hanging from it free, turned away and started to run off.

Trevor Crisp and Flora Carter came running up.

'Stop her,' Angel called.

They caught her in their arms.

'Hold her, but be careful,' Angel called. 'She is probably armed.'

'Are you all right, sir?' they said in unison.

Angel ran up to them and quickly grabbed the hanging handcuff and the free wrist. She fought like the she-cat she was, but eventually he managed to secure the cuffs and fasten them with her arms behind her back.

'Take hold of her, Flora,' Angel said. 'Don't let go.'

Flora Carter grabbed the woman at the back by the cuffs.

Marcia Moore glared at Angel and said, 'You're like all men. Frigging pigs!'

Unmoved at the outburst, Angel looked at her and said, 'Marcia Moore, I am arresting you for the murder of James Argyle, Lee Ellis, Charles Domino and probably Joseph Memoré. You do not have to say anything, but it may harm your defence if you do not mention when questioned, something that you later rely on in court. Anything you do say may be used in evidence.'

Flora's eyes stood out like elderberries on stalks. 'She's the Chameleon, sir?' she said.

Crisp looked as if he had been whacked on the head with a barrister's briefcase. 'I don't believe it,' he said.

Angel said, 'It's true. And she needs to be searched very carefully indeed. I believe you will find one or more stilettos, which will prove it,' he said. 'You'll also probably find the Rosary.'

'Ridiculous,' Marcia Moore said. 'It is Joseph Memoré who was the Chameleon. He was going to murder *me*! You heard him, Mr Angel. He said so, several times.'

Angel shook his head. 'Save it, Miss Moore,' he said. 'You can tell it to the jury.'

A uniformed man carrying a Heckler & Koch rifle, and wearing a gun holster and a helmet with the word POLICE on it, rushed up behind them. It was DI Waldo White of the FSU.

Angel looked up at him and sighed.

White said. 'Is everything all right, Michael? Sorry we're a bit late. To tell the truth, we got lost.'

'Everything's fine,' Angel said without conviction. He noticed two khaki Range Rovers loaded with armed police parked at the kerb. He turned back to White and pointed up to the flat behind him and said, 'There is a man in there, Waldo. He is probably armed. This woman says she shot him and that she thinks he is dead, so I need to get up there fast.'

'We'll see to it, Michael,' White said.

'It was self-defence,' Marcia Moore muttered, her head now bowed. She was shivering and her teeth were rattling. Her eyes resumed the half-closed state. 'Anybody got a cigarette?' she added.

Angel looked at White and said, 'Have you any women in your unit?'

'Yes. Two. Why?'

'This woman is the Chameleon.'

White's jaw dropped open. He stared at Marcia Moore. He couldn't take his eyes off her.

'She needs very careful searching,' Angel said. Then he nodded towards Flora and added, 'With my sergeant, here, do you think you could organize that?'

'Sure,' White said. He turned and waved towards the first Range Rover. A man also wearing protection gear and carrying a rifle came running up. White told the man what was required. He ran back to the Range Rover and the doors of the two vehicles opened and some of the armed police rushed across the yard and swarmed around White. He quietly told them what was required.

At the same time, Angel grabbed Flora by the sleeve and pulled her away from the others. 'Stay with her,' he whispered. 'Don't leave her side until she's in a cell at the station. And if she wants to talk, record everything she says.'

Flora nodded grimly.

An FSU woman escorted Flora and Marcia Moore across to the Range Rover.

'I had to do it,' Marcia Moore whined. 'He would have killed me. Anybody got a cigarette . . . ?'

White turned back to Angel, nodded towards the flat and said, 'Now leave it to us, Michael. He might not be dead, and we have the protection of our body armour.'

White then lead eight armed police up the steps to the flat.

Angel stood at the bottom and waited.

SEVENTEEN

It was 8.28 a.m., on Friday, 16 December 2011.

Angel bustled through the station back door, past the cells, and along the busy main corridor leading from the rear door all the way down to his office. The dozen or so police or civilian staff he passed, without exception, smiled, or nodded or spoke. He beamed as he acknowledged the courtesy. The attention was a little exceptional and was an understood appreciation that he had uncovered the identity of the Chameleon and what's more, that he had her stashed away so that she could not kill again!

He glided into his office, threw his overcoat at the hook on the steel cabinet and slipped into the swivel chair.

There was a knock at the door. It was Ahmed. He came in all smiles. 'Good morning, sir,' he said. 'DS Carter asked me to give this to you.' He put a small pile of coins on Angel's desk. 'It's the change from the cigarettes, sir.'

Angel frowned, picked up the coins, counted them, blew out a foot of breath, looked up at the ceiling and said, 'Good grief. Cigarettes? She must have got her a box of Havanas!'

He put the money in his pocket, turned to Ahmed and said, 'I want to see Don Taylor as soon as he comes in.'

'Right, sir,' he said and he went out.

DS Taylor arrived several minutes later.

'What about Memoré then, Don?'

'Well, sir, subject to anything that Dr Mac may come up with, it's straightforward enough. Memoré was shot once in the chest with the Beretta, which we know from past experience was Memoré's favourite weapon. His prints are all over the shell cases. And Marcia Moore shot him, as she freely admits. Her prints are on the trigger and the butt. There is no forensic to indicate that anybody else was at the scene, before or after the gunshot. So that's about it.'

Angel nodded. 'All nice and tidy.'

'What about the Rosary, sir?' Taylor said. 'Where was it exactly?'

'Flora found it. It was wrapped in a gent's handkerchief and tucked in the top of one of her stockings. In the top of the other stocking was a stiletto. And in a leather sheath sewn inside the collar of her dress was another one.'

Taylor winced. 'Deadly.'

'Evidence enough to convict her of the murders,' Angel said.

Taylor went out.

Angel leaned back in his chair and squeezed the lobe of his ear between his finger and thumb as he went through a mental checklist. He reckoned that he had done everything he could do up to that point to progress the case against Marcia Moore. So he turned round to the table behind his chair and picked up a red file. It was the file with the six transcripts of the interviews between Haydn King and Mrs Lin. It looked like around a hundred and twenty pages of closely typed A4 sheets. He wasn't looking forward to the read. It looked very wordy and uninteresting.

He had to try and get into the mind of Haydn King to try to understand how it was possible that he could repeatedly dream of meeting his death in his swimming pool and then two days later, for the nightmare to become a reality. He also hoped to discover the reason why King had employed actor Reuben Paschal, who had looked so very much like him, also he wanted to know why Paschal appeared to have been shaved after he also was murdered.

There was a knock at the door.

He looked up. 'Come in.'

It was Flora Carter.

'Have you a minute, sir. I've something you'd be interested in.'

Angel was relieved. It delayed him from having to delve into the potentially boring state of Haydn King's mind. He pointed to the chair, then he closed the file, tossed the wadge of A4 back onto the table behind him and turned back to face her.

'Aye,' he said. 'What is it? By the way, has that solicitor arrived for Marcia Moore?'

'He's in the cell with her now, sir.'

'Ah. Good.'

Flora took the seat opposite him.

'I would have thought you would have gone home by now,' he said. 'Catch up with some sleep. You were here with her till very late last night.'

Flora smiled. 'It was all worthwhile, sir. Those cigarettes worked wonders. She'd do anything for a cigarette. Last night she talked almost non-stop. Mostly about men. She doesn't think much to men.'

Angel gave a wry smile. 'Did she confess to anything, or make any admission of any guilt at all?'

'She's too clever to confess to murder directly, sir,' Flora said, taking a tiny audio recorder out of her handbag. 'But she did say something interesting. I thought you'd like to hear it.'

He nodded approvingly.

She put the recorder on his desk and pressed the play button.

Angel closed his eyes as he listened.

The playback was tinny and distorted but it was clearly Marcia Moore's voice.

'I've been used by men all my life, and I thought James Argyle was different. I thought he loved me. I really, really did. I would have done anything for him. We had even agreed to share the money from the sale of the Rosary on a 50/50 basis. But when Charles Domino and Joseph Memoré pretended to threaten to kill me by pushing me out of that hotel window if he didn't give them the Rosary, do you know, he didn't care. He didn't give a damn. He simply let them do it. And he honestly believed that they had killed me. He did. And he still wouldn't tell them what he'd done with the Rosary.

'Charlie Domino, Joseph Memoré and me went out earlier and got two matching suits and coats in my size, a mannequin from a dress shop and some blood from a butcher's to pretend that it was my dead body on the ground in the hotel car park. I honestly didn't think that all that was necessary, but they knew better . . . and they were right! Yes. They *were* right!

'I actually climbed down to the floor below on a rope fastened to a sofa and strung out through the bedroom window. Then after James had seen it, and thought it was me, I had to go outside and shift the mannequin before anybody else saw it. I dumped the whole thing in one of the big hotel waste bins, which were handy. But James Argyle was a pig. A pig! An absolute pig! And Charlie Domino and Joseph Memoré eventually got their own way. Memoré threatened to cut off his ears, his nose and some other bits if he didn't tell them where the Rosary was. And he meant it. James Argyle broke down and told them that the Rosary had been passed on to . . . to somebody else for safe-keeping until the heat was off.'

Flora reached out and switched the recorder off and looked across the desk at Angel. 'There was a lot more, mostly denigrating James Argyle, Charles Domino, Joseph Memoré and men in particular.'

Angel thought a moment and then said, 'Hmm. That was worth knowing, Flora. Great stuff. That puts Harry Wiseman in the clear. And we can add shop breaking and burglary to her charge sheet.'

She gave a small smile. 'I'll go home for a couple of hours, sir . . . if you don't mind?'

'No, lass. You've earned it.'

She went out and Angel returned to the wodge of paper from Mrs Lin. He looked at the front page of the top one. It said: 'Transcript of first interview with Haydn King, The Old Hall, Pine Avenue, Bromersley. 8 p.m. November 1, 2011.' Then he looked at the others. He checked the dates on the title page of each interview and was about to return to the first, when it came to his mind that the date of 6 December 2011 on the last one, was two days before Haydn King was found dead in his swimming pool.

Angel leaned back in the chair. That date reverberated in his mind for a while. December 6th. December 6th. He recalled that it was St Nicholas Day and that that old saint was the model for the character that became known as Father Christmas. But that wasn't it. It was something far removed from that. The date would bug him until he remembered.

He decided to read the last interview, the one dated December 6th, first, as it might save him reading the other five. Then it dawned on him; he suddenly knew the significance of December 6th. That was the date the superintendent had said he had visited Haydn King. And that had also been at eight o'clock in the evening. He pushed back the swivel chair and mooched out of his office across the corridor to the CID room.

Ahmed and two other detectives were in there gazing at their computer screens when Angel went in. They looked up at him. He didn't address them so they continued with their work.

Angel stared across at the whiteboard covering most of one wall of the room. On it were all the known facts of his current cases, dates, times, places, including photographs of Haydn King, Vincent Fleming, Judy Savage, Lee Ellis, Reuben Paschal, James Argyle, Joseph Memoré and Marcia Moore.

Angel frowned when he saw that there was no mention of Superintendent Harker's meeting with Haydn King on December 6th.

Ahmed forsook his computer and came up to him. 'You all right, sir?' he said.

Angel's knuckles tightened. 'That meeting the super had with Haydn King on December 6th isn't up there.'

Ahmed blinked. 'It *was*, sir. But the super saw it and told me to take it down because he said it had nothing to do with the investigation.'

Angel became grim. '*What?*' he bawled.

The other two detectives in the room turned round to see the reason for the outburst. He glared at them and they turned back to their screens.

He exhaled noisily, turned towards the door, stopped, turned back to Ahmed and quietly said, 'Er, right. Er, thank you, lad. Carry on.'

Then he steamed determinedly out of the room.

Ahmed frowned then settled back down at his desk.

Angel stormed straight up the corridor to Superintendent Harker's office. He banged on the door and walked in. He was met by the usual excessive heat and smell of menthol.

He saw Harker at his desk behind a pile of books, ledgers, papers and Kleenex boxes. He looked more ghastly than usual. His head was like a skull with ears.

Harker looked up, sniffed, turned down the corners of his mouth and said, 'It's you, Angel. I was about to send for you.'

He threw his pen down onto the desk. 'Sit down,' he added.

Angel took the chair opposite and glared back at him.

Harker peered between the piles of books, papers and stuff. 'Do you know what rules are for, lad?' he said.

'That's just what I wanted to speak to you about, sir.'

'What?' Harker said, his eyes bigger than gobstoppers. He couldn't believe that Angel had come voluntarily to make his excuses. 'Yes, lad?'

'Yes, sir,' Angel said. 'I have just noticed that your meeting with Haydn King is no longer on the case board in the CID room, and that it was removed on *your* instructions.'

It took Harker a couple of seconds to catch up. 'I thought that you . . . Well, yes. I told PC Ahaz to remove it because it has no bearing on the case. As superintendent of this station, I considered that it was most inappropriate for reasons of discipline to have my name on a case board in company with witnesses, crooks, suspects and dead bodies.'

'But it has a bearing on the case. Also, it would have been appropriate to have told me that you intended removing it. I am supposed to be in charge of the case. Its absence could have resulted in an important fact being overlooked.'

'*Important fact.* What important fact?'

'The fact that you may have the date wrong. On the date that you gave me, Tuesday December 6th, Haydn King apparently had an evening appointment with his psychiatrist, Mrs Lin.'

Harker didn't reply straightaway. He leaned forward to look at his desk diary. He turned several pages back, then a page forward and then muttered, 'Mmm. Tuesday December 6th. Oh dear. It's not entered in here.' He looked round a pile of files and papers at Angel. 'Oh yes. I remember now,' he said. 'It was in the evening, wasn't it? I went there from home. Eight o'clock. Yes. Well, lad, if I *said* it was that Tuesday evening, Angel, it *was* that Tuesday evening.'

Angel rubbed his chin. 'That means that his psychiatrist is in error, sir.'

'Obviously,' Harker said. 'Go and sort it out with her.'

Angel shook his head. He stood up to go. Harker waved a hand directing him to sit back down.

'Just one moment. I have something to say to you. It is something very important. I thought that that was what you were coming in to explain.'

Angel's forehead made more lines than there are on a charge sheet. 'Explain, sir?'

'Yes. There are eighty-six of them in this station. There are two in reception. One in the briefing room. One in this, the CID room. One in this office. One in each cell. I do believe there is one in your office . . .'

Angel shook his head, then suddenly his face brightened and he said, 'Fire extinguishers, sir?'

Harker's face went as red as the positive light on a breathalyser. 'I'm not referring to fire extinguishers, lad. I'm talking about "No Smoking" signs.'

Angel nodded as it came to him what the superintendent, in his circuitous route, was alluding to. He pursed his lips and waited for the onslaught.

Harker said, 'It came to my notice last night as I looked in on the prisoner, Marcia Moore, that she was smoking a cigarette. And she was sitting not three feet away from a "No Smoking" sign. I asked the duty jailer what he thought he was doing allowing the prisoner to smoke, and he told me that you had not only authorized it, but that that you had actually bought the cigarettes for the prisoner, and a full box of matches, and sent them in.'

Angel knew there was no chance of winning this argument. He decided to keep *shtum* and sit it out.

Harker, having got his second wind, continued: 'So there was a prisoner in a cell in my station, being in possession of a banned tobacco substance, supplied by a senior officer. And not only that, she was also in possession of a box of matches, another banned item, an item capable of burning the station down. What would I have said if the Inspector of Constabulary had called in unexpectedly? How would I have got out of that?'

Angel realized that Harker now wanted his involvement, so he would have to give some sort of an answer. 'I don't know,' he said. 'I have never known an Inspector of Constabulary come down to the cells before introducing himself to the Chief Constable and—'

'What are you babbling on about, lad?'

'It was a quick way to ease the accused into making admissions and explanations that has saved us a *lot* of time, sir. A *lot* of time. And as you say, time is money. I remember when I smoked, it was a great help when I was under stress, and if I had had my cigarettes taken away from me—'

'I don't want to know about your troubles, lad. I don't need a lecture on addiction. You will have to learn to live according to the rules, and the rule in this nick, in the cars and in the car park is, no smoking. And that applies to all ranks and all visitors regardless of whoever they are. Got it?'

'Yes, sir. Got it.'

'Right. Now buzz off and find out what your Mrs Lin has to hide.'

Mrs Lin smiled delightfully as she came into her sitting room, but Angel sensed some resentment of him hidden beneath the charming manner.

He stood up. She gestured to him to sit down, and she sat down opposite him.

'Now then, Inspector. I am with a patient, but we haven't started yet. I can give you two minutes only. What is it that is so important?'

'Hopefully, that's all it will take,' he said.

From his briefcase, he produced the file of transcripts of the interviews with Haydn King and took out the bottom one. He pointed to the top page. 'This is dated 6th December. It was a Tuesday. Is this correct? Are you sure it wasn't the day before, or even the day after?'

She looked at the page. Her expression didn't change. 'I'll get my secretary.'

She went out of the room. She was only away a few seconds. She returned with a young woman who was carrying a large slim book.

'This is Inspector Angel, Amina,' Mrs Lin said. 'Please point out to him the entry of Mr King's appointment.'

Amina held the book over his shoulder. It was an appointment diary showing a week at a time and she was holding it open at the first week in December. It confirmed what Mrs Lin had said. The name 'Haydn King' appeared on the 8 p.m. line under the date Tuesday, December 6, 2011.

It was a clean and tidy handwritten entry. There didn't seem to be any alteration, rubbing out or inking over.

Angel stood up and said, 'Well, yes, thank you. That seems clear enough.'

'Thank you, Amina,' Mrs Lin said, also standing. 'Please tell my next patient I will only be a moment.'

Amina closed the book and went out.

Mrs Lin said, 'I hope you are satisfied. And now, dear Inspector Angel, I have to go.'

Angel said, 'I have to ask you this, Mrs Lin. It is extremely important. Even so, is there any possible chance that you could be mistaken?'

'Absolutely not,' she said.

'On Tuesday evening, December 6th last, between 8 p.m. and 9 p.m., Mr Haydn King was here and you were with him?'

'Indeed I was. Now I really must go, Inspector. Please see yourself out. Excuse me.'

Angel returned to the station. He sat in his office rubbing his chin and thinking about his next move in the case.

He reached out for the phone and tapped in a number. It was soon answered.

'Yes, sir,' Ahmed said.

'There's a psychiatrist, a Mrs Lin, lives at 2 Pine Close. Contact CRO, see if anything is known. And ring me straight back.'

'Right, sir.'

He then rang his GP and managed to speak to him. The doctor said that he knew Mrs Lin, he spoke very highly of the woman and said that he referred patients to her from time to time, preferring her to the only other specialist he knew of in the town. Angel thanked him and replaced the phone. Then he dialled his old friend and colleague Dr Mac.

'Well, laddie, Jennifer Lin is the best in the business. Known her years. I can highly recommend her. And, by the way, she would make you an excellent witness.'

Angel's eyebrows shot up. That was praise indeed. 'Thank you, Mac,' he said.

Minutes later, Ahmed phoned back. 'Nothing known about Mrs Lin, sir.'

Angel knew that he should be cheered by the positive reports on the woman, but they indicated that Harker had to be wrong. And going back and arguing the point further with him would not exactly be enjoyable.

This was at the forefront of his mind when he arrived home at 5.30 that cold Friday night. Over poached salmon, new potatoes and peas he explained the problem to Mary.

'The super insists that it was Tuesday, 6th December when Haydn King summoned him, the super, to King's house and told him about the dream where King saw himself floating dead in his swimming pool. Mrs Lin, his highly respectable psychiatrist, insists that Haydn King was consulting her in her surgery on the same evening and at the same time. Clearly, one of them has to be wrong,' he said as he helped himself to more potatoes.

Mary said, 'Well, the super isn't getting any younger.'

'Huh! He should be pensioned off, but he won't go.'

'And he's not very well, is he? What's his memory like?'

'All right . . . I think.'

'That might be the problem,' she said. 'He's forgotten and he's simply got the date mixed up.'

'But he's adamant it was Tuesday, 6th. As is Mrs Lin. This means I must be overlooking something, Mary. I am going to have to re-evaluate all the evidence and look at the case from an entirely different angle.'

'Has the super anything to gain from insisting it was the 6th?'

Angel considered the point as he eased the salmon off the skin. 'Mmm. I don't think so, love. Don't know of anything.'

'It seems to me that the only other possibility is that the super is trying to establish an alibi for himself, for some reason.'

He thought about what Mary had said. It seemed to him that she was suggesting that Harker might be engaged in something unlawful. He promptly dismissed it. But in the absence of any other explanation, the idea lingered in his subconscious.

They finished the meal, retired to the sitting room for coffee and when she had served it, she said, 'It's a week to Christmas Eve, tomorrow, you know. We must put the tree up . . . and the lights . . . and the trimmings.'

And so the weekend was committed to preparing for the coming celebration.

Throughout Saturday and Sunday, Angel did everything that Mary asked of him, but the idea of Harker being engaged in something dishonest created a turmoil in his mind and even when he was sticking the Christmas cards to long strips of paper to make them convenient to hang, his mind was still occupied thinking about Mrs Lin, Haydn King, Reuben Paschal and the swimming pool. It was the same when he was watching *Songs of Praise* followed by repeats of re-runs of clips from old *Carry On* films.

Mary watched him surreptitiously throughout that Sunday evening. She noticed his half-closed eyes and the hand either caressing his chin or tapping lightly on the arm of the chair and knew his mind was still on the case.

He was still thinking about it when he had got into bed, kissed Mary, switched off the light and pulled the duvet around his shoulders.

'It'll soon be Christmas. Have a good night, sweetheart,' Mary said.

He smiled although she could not see it. 'You must remember to put your stocking up,' he said.

She giggled.

The last thing he remembered before dropping off to sleep was Mary saying, 'And don't be thinking about that Haydn King business all night.'

'Goodnight, darling,' he murmured.

EIGHTEEN

Angel was suddenly wide awake. His eyes clicked open. He glanced around the bedroom. It was as black as fingerprint ink.

He eased himself up from the pillows and peered through the dark at the bedside table. The glowing hands of the clock told him that it was either 7.20 or 3.35.

He blinked, then yawned.

And *that* was the Eureka moment!

That's when it all happened. That's when he knew who had murdered Haydn King and Reuben Paschal. He also knew why the super persisted in his claim that Haydn King had told him about the nightmare at eight o'clock on the evening of the 6th December, when Angel knew that it was not possible.

Angel had committed the basic mistake of making an assumption. It was all to do with the Astra Agency. Now that his subconscious had overridden his supposition, allowing his mind to explore all the options, it had found the only one that perfectly fitted the situation, and — hey presto! — out had popped the explanation. The mystery was solved. His mind then darted from one point to the next, finding explanations of all the details that had previously baffled him.

Everything was now as clear to him as a bottle of Booth's.

But he had to prove the case. Absolutely essential so that he could wrap it up, pass it on to the CPO and have a tranquil Christmas at home with the ever-delightful Mary, untroubled by more demanding murder inquiries.

Proving the case in a court of law might be difficult. Then it came to him.

He believed that there was conclusive evidence in the locked bedroom of Mrs Lydia King, the late mother of Haydn King, that would put away the murderer of Haydn King and Reuben Paschal for life.

His heart thumped as solidly and regularly as the big drum in the Salvation Army. He was over the moon, and he simply could not stay in bed, but he didn't want to wake Mary. He listened motionless for a few seconds to her slow, regular breathing, then gently peeled back the duvet. He found his dressing-gown, went downstairs and made himself a drink of tea in a beaker. He brought it back upstairs and went quietly into the bathroom. He was soon shaved, washed and dressed. He left a note for Mary under the magnet on the fridge door and went out.

It was 8.30 a.m. and Angel had been in his office at Bromersley Police Station for more than two hours, busy writing up the case for Mr Twelvetrees of the CPS in his quest to put the two current cases to bed and have his desk clear by Christmas Eve.

He looked at his watch. It was 8.35 a.m. He reached out for the phone and tapped in the number of the SOCO office.

DS Taylor answered.

Angel said, 'Pick up your bag, Don, and meet me at the rear door. I want you to come with me. I think the key that will lead us to the murderer of Haydn King and Reuben Paschal lies in Mrs Lydia King's bedroom. I need to get in there to solve this mystery.'

'Right, sir.'

Ten minutes later Angel was driving the BMW along Pine Avenue, through the wrought-iron gates into the grounds of the mansion of the late Haydn King. As he swerved round the bend in the drive and passed the screen of lime trees he saw a man on a bicycle pedalling along in front. The cyclist must have heard the approach of the BMW because he pulled over to the left and waved the car on.

As Angel overtook him, he recognized the rider.

'It's Mark Rogers,' Taylor said. 'Presumably going to work.'

Angel said, 'And if he's chauffeuring for Vincent Fleming, he's late.' He rubbed his chin, then added, 'Funny, isn't it, incongruous, a chauffeur going to work on a bike?'

Taylor smiled wryly.

Angel parked the BMW at the front of the house, and the two men got out. Taylor went round to the car boot and took out his big yellow bag containing sterile sample containers, fingerprinting equipment and other forensic paraphernalia.

Meanwhile Rogers caught up with the car, stopped and said, 'If you are looking for Mr Fleming, Inspector, he'll be out at the moment. He will have gone to his office in town. But he'll be back later this morning, though, I expect. Anything I can help you with?'

'Not just yet, Mr Rogers,' Angel said. 'Not just yet. Thank you.'

The chauffeur frowned, then pressing down on the cycle pedal with one foot and pushing himself off the gravel with the other, he rode off to the end of the house and round to the garages.

Angel and Taylor then went up the steps to the front door and rang the bell.

They waited for what seemed to be a long time. It was suddenly opened by Mrs Johnson who was red in the face and panting. She looked at them, disappointed. 'Oh it's only you,' she said. 'Good heavens. Who do you want to see?'

Behind her, Meredith came rushing into view. He looked down at the chubby housekeeper as if she was a fly in the cookhouse slop bucket at Strangeways. 'I was just coming, Mrs Johnson. There was no need for you to attend.'

She glared at back him and rushed away.

Meredith turned to Angel and Taylor and said, 'Good morning, gentlemen. Sorry about that. Mr Fleming is out at the moment. Can I be of service?'

'Yes,' Angel said. 'We want to take another look in Lady Lydia's bedroom. Would you unlock it for us?'

'Of course, sir. Please come in.'

As they crossed the hall, Harry Saw came out of the study carrying a briefcase the size of a Black Maria and almost ran into them.

'I do beg your pardon,' Saw said, taking a backward step.

'That's all right,' Taylor said.

Angel's eyes narrowed as he watched Saw hurry across the parquet floor lugging the heavy briefcase towards the front door.

Meredith pressed the button to summon the lift and took Angel and Taylor up the one flight.

At the door of Lady Lydia's bedroom, Meredith produced his keys, unlocked the door, opened it and followed the other two gentlemen inside. 'Will you be long, sir?'

'I am not sure,' Angel said.

'Well, please ring when you've finished. There's a bell push at the side of the bed.'

'Thank you, Mr Meredith.'

He went out and closed the door.

It was almost an hour later that Angel rang the bell while Taylor finished packing up his bag of forensic samples and equipment and closing the zip.

Angel looked pleased with himself as he looked round the room to check that everything was tidy and in place.

Meredith tapped lightly on the door and came in. 'Have you finished, sir, and is everything satisfactory?'

'Yes, thank you, Mr Meredith,' Angel said.

The door suddenly opened and Vincent Fleming came in. He glared at each of the three men in turn. His eyes were bright and piercing, his face pastier than usual.

'What's happening, Meredith?' he said.

'The Inspector expressed a wish to take a further look at Lady Lydia's room, sir,' the butler said. 'He has just finished and the two gentlemen were about to leave.'

Fleming looked at Angel and said, 'I hope you have everything you need now, Inspector Angel. I can't have you popping in and out of my house whenever you feel like it, as if it was a railway station.'

Angel breathed in and filled his lungs. He pursed his lips, then said, 'The investigation into your uncle's death is now completed so I don't think that will be necessary. Good day.'

Vincent Fleming's jaw dropped.

Taylor picked up his bag and the two policemen went out of the room and down the stairs. They let themselves out of the front door and made straight for the BMW and Bromersley Police Station.

When they arrived at Angel's office door, he turned to Taylor and said, 'Let me have those results as soon as you can, Don.'

'Yes, of course, sir,' Taylor said and he disappeared down the corridor.

Angel went into his office. And as he took off his overcoat, without realizing it, and for no explicable reason, he began to whistle *The Teddy Bears' Picnic.*

There was a knock on the door. He stopped whistling. It was Ahmed. 'Good morning, sir. Did you know the super was looking for you earlier?'

Angel's face creased. It wasn't news he enjoyed hearing. He sighed and said, 'Right, lad. I had better go up then.'

'He's not in now, sir. He got an urgent call from that costume hire place at the back of the Town Hall.'

Angel looked up into Ahmed's eyes. He was thinking that it must be something really serious to cause the superintendent to attend personally.

'Why, what's happened?' he said earnestly. He could see his quiet Christmas at home in jeopardy.

'I understand that it's to try on a Father Christmas suit for the children's party, sir,' Ahmed said.

Angel's mouth dropped open.

Suddenly the office door opened and Superintendent Harker himself appeared in overcoat, scarf and hat, his nose glowing redder than usual. He looked round, saw Ahmed, and ignored him, then he saw Angel and his eyebrows shot up.

'Ah, Angel,' Harker began. '*There* you are. Have you been looking for me?'

'No, sir.'

Harker frowned. 'Oh? Had to go out. Something very urgent arose. Come on up. I want a word.'

'Right, sir,' Angel said.

Harker went out, leaving the door open.

Ahmed grinned, looked at Angel and said, 'Do you want me for anything, sir?'

Angel saw his face, but he wasn't amused. 'No, lad,' he said. 'Buzz off. You'd still be laughing if your backside was on fire, wouldn't you?'

'Yes, sir. No, sir. I don't know, sir,' he said in quick succession.

'Get out of it,' Angel growled.

Ahmed went out, laughing quietly.

Angel switched off the desk light, closed the office door and made his way up the corridor.

'Come in, lad,' Harker said as he dragged off his scarf. 'Sit down.'

There was the sound of a click followed by a tinny rattle and a waft of air as he switched on the antique convector heater he kept out of sight under the desk.

'It'll soon warm up.'

Angel considered it quite warm enough.

Harker hung his hat and coat on a hanger in a locker behind his chair and sat down behind the cluttered desk. 'Now we can get on,' he said.

The superintendent was being so remarkably polite and affable that Angel peered at him and wondered what he was up to.

Harker rubbed his chin then said, 'Erm, so, that woman, Mrs Lin. You went to see her again?'

'Yes, sir. In view of our discussion, I had to.'

'And erm, what did she say?'

Angel said, 'I was shown the entry of the appointment of Haydn King in the appointment diary. It *was* at that same time and date that *you* said you were with him.'

Harker frowned. He rubbed his chin. 'And so I was. An entry in a book proves nowt, lad.'

'That's right, sir, but the point is that she had spoken to him several times before and knew him, whereas you didn't know him.'

'What are getting at, lad?'

'Well, it was not Haydn King you saw that night, sir. You were deliberately fooled by an actor, Reuben Paschal.'

Harker blinked several times. 'But I had a letter from King, I was shown into his study, in his house, by his butler. He told me confidentially about his recurrent dream.'

'It was a set-up, sir. It was a plot, conceived by Angel's butler, Nicholas Fitzroy Meredith and carried out by him with the assistance of Reuben Paschal, an out-of-work actor who had a record. Clever, don't you think, to involve a senior police officer and plant the totally fictitious tale about a repeated nightmare *before* the murder so that when the victim's body was found, "suicide while the balance of his mind . . ." would immediately be thought to be a factor in the cause of death?'

Harker was thoroughly annoyed. He screwed up his face and said, 'You are barking up the wrong tree, lad.'

'Paschal was a similar build to King and had a distinguished black beard. At a distance one could easily be mistaken for the other. You had never met King before, sir, had you?'

Harker blinked then said, 'Well, er no.'

'So you wouldn't know that it *wasn't* Haydn King you were seeing. You see, Meredith knew that King was changing his will in his favour. But also knowing how fickle King was, he wanted to be sure of inheriting before King changed his will back again. He knew that he had an appointment at his solicitor's on Monday to sign the new will. However, he had assumed, wrongly as it happened, that he kept the appointment. You see, that was the day King had a touch of gout, so he cried off and went to the doctor's instead. Meredith wasn't to know that that attack of gout caused Haydn King to cancel his appointment with his solicitor, so the will remained in favour of his nephew, Vincent Fleming, and King's millions were never to come to within Meredith's grasp.

'It was Meredith who phoned the Astra Agency, having selected Paschal from their website online because he looked similar to King.'

Harker sniffed, his watery eyes wavered like a needle in a marine compass as he listened attentively.

'For a while,' Angel said, 'I thought it was King who had engaged the actor as his double for some reason, and it threw me completely off the track. Anyway, we learned from his sister that Paschal was desperately hard up and that he had told her that the new job would enable him to buy his own place and set himself up for the future.

'King was actually killed by being struck on the head with a common or garden house brick. There are minuscule fragments in the wound. I believe the injury was intended to simulate an injury he might have suffered had he dived badly and landed on his head on the pool edge. But the murder was actually executed in King's bedroom, probably while he was asleep. There is some brick dust there, and forensic supports this. Then the two men changed King into his swimming trunks, transferred him to his late mother's wheelchair, transported him in the lift down to the swimming pool and tipped him in. A book about dreams was placed at the side of his bed by Meredith to persuade us that King was greatly disturbed by the nightmares he was supposed to be having. His prints and the prints of Mrs Selina Johnson, the housekeeper, are on it, but not King's, which was obviously significant. And that's what made me first suspect Meredith.

'After the murder, Meredith saw Paschal out of the house then phoned triple nine. However, a few days later, when Paschal found out King's inheritance would go to his nephew, Vincent Fleming, he realized that he would not be paid the fortune promised and that he had been involved in a pointless murder. He may have threatened to go to the police if Meredith didn't cough up. Who knows? But they must have had the most rancorous quarrel. So much so that it seemed necessary to Meredith to dispose of Paschal before he was betrayed by him. So he killed Paschal in the same way he killed Haydn King. Then, when he was dead, because Paschal looked so much like King, he hastily cut off his beard so that we would not notice the similarity. Then in the night, Meredith transferred the body . . . using the wheelchair again . . . into the boot of one of King's cars and drove him to the canal and dumped him there. I expect to have confirmation shortly that the tread of one of the wheelchair tyres, which we thought was from a bicycle, matches the track left in the mud at the side of the canal where the body was tipped in, also that there are recent fingerprints of Meredith on the wheelchair. There are minute particles of a house brick in the skulls of both King and Paschal, the wounds are approximately in the centre of the skulls, and they were both dumped in water after they had been killed. I believe that the case against Meredith for the murder of Paschal will then be conclusive, and, as the MO is exactly the same, the jury will bring in a verdict of guilty against Meredith for King's murder as well.'

Harker nodded, then frowned and said, 'How could Meredith be certain that King would be out of the house when I called?'

'King had kept five consecutive weekly appointments at Mrs Lin's on Tuesdays at 8, why wouldn't he keep the sixth? There's something else, sir. Haydn King was a proud man. He didn't want it known that he had need to seek the services of a psychiatrist, and a woman psychiatrist at that. He didn't even make an entry in his appointments diary for prying eyes to read. But he told one person, the one person he thought he could trust, his butler. King would have had to tell him, to avoid being locked out of the house and so that he knew what time to serve his bedtime cocoa or whatever.'

Harker nodded.

Angel continued. 'So Meredith chose that date and time, confident that nobody knew he was consulting a psychiatrist. However, Haydn King phoned Mrs Lin on his mobile on Thursday, December 1st. We don't know what the call was about, but if my team hadn't followed up her number and I hadn't interviewed the lady, we might never have discovered the truth.'

Harker held out his hands, his fingertips touching intermittently in a rhythm only he would have understood. His half-open eyes looked downward, but saw nothing. 'You'd better get a warrant and get Meredith arrested,' he said.

Angel looked up at him and said, 'It's in hand, sir. Got a warrant from Dr Leigh and I've sent a patrol car to pick him up.'

Harker blinked. 'Mmm. I hope we are not going to be housing and feeding him for long.'

'I completed the paperwork earlier this morning, sir. He can go up before the magistrates this morning and be away to Armley or Durham tomorrow.'

'And he can stay there until the new year. Good riddance. What about Marcia Moore, when are we getting shot of her?'

'GSL are collecting her anytime now, sir, for New Hall.'

Harker nodded approvingly. 'All nice and tidy for Christmas. You'd better crack on, then, lad,' he said.

Angel came out of the superintendent's office and made his way down the corridor in time to hear the shrill sound of a female voice from the direction of the cells. It was Marcia Moore.

'What's all this?' she was yelling. 'I don't want to wear *those* again. They hurt my bloody wrists. Don't push. What's happening?'

'You're being moved to New Hall,' a female voice replied.

Angel recognized the voice was that of PC Leisha Baverstock.

'What for? Where's that?' Marcia Moore said.

'It's a woman's prison, about ten miles away.'

'Oh. I don't want to go. I don't want to go. I am not going.'

'You have to go, Marcia. And you'll be far better off. It's in the countryside. You'll be better off there, Marcia. They have far more facilities than there are here.'

'Oh? I hope there's a shop there. Anybody got a cigarette? I say, anybody got a cigarette?'

Angel reached his office. He closed the door and returned to his desk. He had just sat down when the phone rang.

It was Taylor. 'You'll be pleased to know, sir, that Meredith's fingerprints were all over the wheelchair, and that the tread on the right-hand tyre matched exactly the track mark we found at the side of the canal.'

'Great stuff, Don. Write it up and let me have it ASAP.'

He returned the phone to its holster and leaned back in the swivel chair, a warm smile on his face. He was thinking that he would be able to pass on all the case notes to Mr Twelvetrees, the barrister, at the CPS on Wednesday, 21st, in two days' time, and that would allow him Thursday and Friday to clear his desk of the accumulation of the paperwork of the past two weeks, leaving everything straight for Christmas. He would be able to rest easy and enjoy Christmas at home with Mary.

He looked at the pile of papers on the desk in front of him needing his attention. He leaned forward and pulled them towards him. He was about to start riffling through them when the phone rang. He reached out for it. It was Harker.

'I've just had a triple nine, lad,' he said. 'A man has been found dead in a flat with what looks like a shotgun wound. The address is . . .'

Angel sighed and reached for his pen.

THE END

OTHER BOOKS BY ROGER SILVERWOOD

YORKSHIRE MURDER MYSTERIES

Book 1: THE MISSING NURSE
Book 2: THE MISSING WIFE
Book 3: THE MAN IN THE PINK SUIT
Book 4: THE MORALS OF A MURDERER
Book 5: THE AUCTION MURDERS
Book 6: THE MISSING KILLER
Book 7: THE UMBRELLA MURDERS
Book 8: THE MISSING MILLIONAIRE
Book 9: THE MISSING THIEF
Book 10: FIND THE LADY
Book 11: THE MISSING MODEL
Book 12: MURDER IN BARE FEET
Book 13: THE MISSING HUSBAND
Book 14: THE CUCKOO CLOCK MURDERS
Book 15: SHRINE TO MURDER
Book 16: THE SNUFFBOX MURDERS
Book 17: THE DOG COLLAR MURDERS
Book 18: THE CHESHIRE CAT MURDERS
Book 19: THE DIAMOND ROSARY MURDERS

FREE KINDLE BOOKS AND OFFERS

Please join our mailing list for free Kindle crime thriller, detective, mystery, and romance books and new releases, as well as news on Roger's next book!
www.joffebooks.com/contact

Thank you for reading this book. If you enjoyed it please leave feedback on Amazon, and if there is anything we missed or you have a question about then please get in touch. The author and publishing team appreciate your feedback and time reading this book.

Our email is office@joffebooks.com

www.joffebooks.com

Follow us on Facebook, Twitter and Instagram
@joffebooks

We hate typos too but sometimes they slip through.
Please send any errors you find to
corrections@joffebooks.com
We'll get them fixed ASAP. We're very grateful to eagle-eyed readers who take the time to contact us.

Printed in Great Britain
by Amazon

83619018R00123